✳ *Christmas* ✳
IN EVERGREEN

Based on the Hallmark Channel Original Movie

D1173441

NANCY NAIGLE

Print ISBN: 978-1-947892-25-5
Ebook ISBN: 978-1-947892-24-8

www.hallmarkpublishing.com
For more about the movie visit:
www.hallmarkchannel.com/a-christmas-in-evergreen

Table of Contents

Chapter One

On northern Vermont—so far north that on clear days you might be able to see the North Pole—lies the magical town of Evergreen. A snowy town all done up for Christmas with a tree in the town square right next to the gazebo, and festive decorations on every single building.

And Evergreen takes Christmas seriously, all year round. Even the sign at the edge of town has jolly old St. Nick waving a welcome to every visitor. From there, it's just a short drive through the rustic covered bridge, then a lovely mountain ride down the only road into town.

Some say it's the decorations that make this little town so special. But others believe it's because of something else entirely...something you wouldn't expect at all...a snow globe.

Yes. A very special snow globe.

Where would one find this magical snow globe, you might ask?

Right on Main Street in the Chris Kringle Kitchen,

a family-owned diner with a yuletide spin. It's the heart of this town, always filled with the locals. Outside, the sign boasts CHRIS KRINGLE KITCHEN in bold red letters with candy cane trim and Santa carrying his sack full of toys and waving. The inside of the diner is just as festive as the outside, and the snow globe…well, it's right there near the front door on the counter next to the cash register, where everyone has access to it.

In its place of honor, a raised platform surrounded by fresh evergreen, the snow globe gets a lot of attention from everyone who passes through the doors.

The globe's wintery scene is exquisite. A horse-drawn sleigh holds a cozy couple tucked beneath a blanket. The woman's scarf trails behind her in the air as the horse trots through the snowy valley. The brown horse looks strong and fast, and his red harness matches the red-and-green sleigh. The actual glass water globe with the miniature version of Evergreen inside rises from between snow-tipped Christmas trees. The whole scene sits atop the hand-carved wooden base, ready to be shaken. A sign in a pretty frame reads, "Make a Christmas Wish…But Only if You Know What Your Heart Really Wants."

But this wasn't just any snow globe. No, they say that if you shake this one just so… And make one wish, the true wish of your heart, Christmas magic will make it come true.

Now, I know what you're thinking. Could a snow globe really grant wishes?

Well, maybe the story of Christmas in Evergreen will help you believe.

Most of the year, the town of Evergreen could be called the Emerald City for all its glorious greenery. The pine, spruce, fir, and holly dot the landscape in a hundred shades of green. But as the seasons change and the holidays near, everything is blanketed in snow and the town gets dressed in all its traditional finery, turning the snowy Main Street with its quaint shops into the idyllic Christmas spot.

From the cheerful ribbons on each lamppost to the lighted garland along the eaves of every single storefront, shiny, oversized ornaments in red, green, and gold dangle from the garland and match the decorations in the giant wreaths hung between each shop. Fresh pine roping weaves through the white porch railing in front of the professional offices across the street from the post office, continuing the festive look from one end of Main Street clear down to the other.

Today the snow fell in big, fluffy flakes as people hurried along with their glossy shopping bags, going about their last-minute business the week before Christmas.

"Hey, everyone. Here we come." Allie Shaw stepped out of the exam room of her clinic, carrying a basket of six-week-old puppies in for their first checkup. Pug puppies, to be specific. Three in all. Two solid-black females and a boy, bigger than the others, in the more typical fawn color. Their velvety button ears hung against their broad foreheads, accenting those big bug eyes. Absolutely adorable, from their wrinkled faces right down to their curling tails.

Hannah, Allie's friend and the owner of the pups, sat in the chair directly facing the examination room. These puppies were just as cute as the Christmas sweater she was wearing. That gal loved Christmas more than anyone Allie knew.

Allie's next two furry, four-legged patients were already waiting for their appointments.

Teddy, a hyper terrier who'd jump straight from his owner's arms to the examination table doing tricks for a treat before she even got the door closed, perked his ears, looking back at his owner in hopes it was his turn now. Mandy Miller, the town's cat lady, sat on the other side of Hannah, clutching a red pet kennel. Allie could barely see the orange tabby cat backed into the corner of the small carrier. Less than happy about being trapped, the feral cat wasn't shy about letting the world know how he felt about it. The overconfident meowing could probably be heard next door. Allie had no doubt this was another stray that needed to be fixed. It seemed like all stray cats eventually made it over to Mandy's house. She'd already told Mandy this was the last day she was taking patients. Everyone had been squeezing in vet visits before she left. She knew Dr. Myers wouldn't be as generous with the neutering fee as she was, which was too bad, because Mandy really was trying to do a good deed at her own expense.

Allie gave them both a quick smile and then said to Hannah, "Okay, these guys have got their shots and are ready for their first Christmas."

Hannah jumped from her chair and raced over to see her puppies, giving them each a rub on the forehead.

This was the part of the job Allie never tired of. She loved having her own practice. Sure, there were days when difficult things had to be taken care of and she turned into a veterinarian and owner therapist all-in-one, but even those days she knew she'd done her best to help a family through the situation they'd been dealt.

Allie handed the large oval wicker basket of pugs over to Hannah.

Hugging the basket to herself, Hannah couldn't help but smile and coo. "Awwww. I can't get over how cute they are!"

"How's our new momma doing?" Allie had given Molly her puppy shots two years ago and had been her doctor ever since. She'd be lying' if she said it didn't make her a little sad to be handing over the medical needs of her patients to someone else now. It was like leaving best friends behind for summer break in elementary school. Only forever.

"Molly definitely has her paws full with these guys." Hannah blew kisses to the pups between words as she moved over in front of the Christmas tree to put some distance between herself and the noisy cat.

Too bad Allie didn't have her camera handy. This would've been the perfect photo op with Hannah holding the puppies next to the clinic's animal-themed Christmas tree with the paw print paper-chain garland. Well, there was a hoof print or two in there, as well. All of her patients participated in that tradition. Even Rhoda the Rhode Island Red hen, who'd broken her wing in a scrape with the neighbor's dog over at Henry Holloway's farm, had a link in the chain. After they'd bandaged Rhoda up, Allie and Henry had dipped her foot in white water-based paint and pressed it down on a pretty red strip of colored paper, leaving the recognizable peace sign prints. That was the first chicken print Allie'd ever had the pleasure of incorporating into her garland. Just paper and staples, but she loved adding to the memories each year.

Allie walked over to the front desk and updated the chart with the next follow-up appointments.

"They sure are going to miss you." Hannah's voice was almost sad.

"I'll miss them, too." It was hard to imagine life away from this clinic and these animals she knew so well. "I'm going to miss *all* my furry patients." *Their parents, too.*

"Wait a minute. You won't have any furry patients in DC?"

Allie made her way from the front desk back to Hannah. "No, I will, but I'm going to be working in a big clinic. I don't know if I'll have time for a pile of pugs." She lifted the tan puppy from the basket and held him in the air. Now she wouldn't even see these little guys grow up. In the clinic the size of the one she was going to work for, she might not have a history with any of the patients like she did here. They had assistants who did routine checks. It would definitely be different.

"Aren't you going to miss it?" Hannah asked.

The tan puppy whimpered and wiggled. Allie's heart swelled. These compact pups were strong and a lot of dog in a little space. She'd have named this little hunk of love Brutus if he was hers.

I'm so lucky to have a job I love so much. How could anything be better than this? She shook the worry from creeping in. She'd miss her small practice, but she was also eager to embrace the possibilities ahead.

"Of course I will, but this is a big opportunity. I can't pass it up." Allie took in a steadying breath. Was she trying to convince Hannah or herself? She'd miss girls' nights out with Hannah and the gang, too. It wasn't easy leaving Evergreen, but she had to give it a try. Grandpa had always said there was a big world out there. It would be a shame not to experience it for herself. She'd spent her whole life in this town, except for those few years she'd gone away to college. How would she ever know where she belonged if she stayed here in Evergreen? "And you've got Dr. Myers's number and info in Montpelier, right?"

"Yep."

"He's great." The puppy squirmed in Allie's hands and then locked gazes with her as if trying to convince her to stay.

"Yes, he is, but..." Hannah shook her head and then whispered, "It's going to be different."

"I know." Allie put the puppy back in the basket with his sisters. "But different is good. Right? Like having a whole bunch of puppies is different, and that's a good thing, right?"

Hannah shrugged and turned her attention back to the puppies. "Yeah, I can't wait to find these guys a new home." The woman made her way to the door. "Bye, Allie."

Allie leaned forward on the desk, peering into the goldfish bowl there. "Now, we just have to find a home for you, Frank."

She was half tempted to bag Frank up and move him with her, but that seemed silly for a dime-store goldfish. She'd had at least twelve Franks over the years, replacing them as they died of old age. Besides, Mom would enjoy taking care of Frank. He might even end up by the magic snow globe on the counter at the diner. That wouldn't be so bad. Although, it did kind of make her wish she'd sprung for the little castle or treasure chest for his bowl now.

Allie finished the other patients. Just as she'd suspected, the cat was a stray. She gave the cat a checkup and its shots, then scheduled the surgery for the day she got back from DC. Allie was quite certain Dr. Meyer would charge more than she had for the procedure, but Allie wanted to help reduce the problem of unwanted kittens. If Mandy Miller was kind enough to capture the feral cats, the least she could do was make it affordable for her to do the good, and responsible, deed.

With the waiting room finally cleared out, she tidied the examination room, filed all the paperwork, and then checked her list to be sure she hadn't forgotten anything. Everything on her list was marked off, except for Frank.

She glanced over at the goldfish. He was content in his glass fishbowl, swimming among the bright blue rocks and dipping behind the anacharis on those days when Frank was feeling shy.

There'd still be a lot to do when she got home after Christmas. This trip this week was just to sign the lease on her new apartment. Well, that and spend Christmas with Spencer there. They'd be attending a few Christmas parties, and he was excited to show her the city Christmas lights. Then it would be back home to do the final preparations for the big moving day.

She'd done a pretty good job getting the house packed so the movers could come and pick up everything the week before she started her new job. Boxes were stacked in every room of her house, but here at the office… She hadn't even begun to liquidate all her pet supplies. The new practice wasn't interested in her bringing any inventory along, so she still had a lot to do.

Finally, there was Frank. He needed be tended

to while she was away. She cleaned out his bowl and then put his food in her pocket, then called the Chris Kringle Kitchen to let her parents know she was on her way down with Frank.

Even though the diner was a short walk—just a few stores up the block and across the street—the bitter Vermont temperatures and snow required bundling up. She took off her white lab coat and hung it on the rack. Her grandmother had embroidered her name on this coat as a graduation gift, and she'd worn it every day since. The new practice required that they all wear the lab coats provided for them with the corporate logo, and a couple of vendor patches. The idea of sponsors seemed weird to her, but that was big business for you.

She took her red wool coat down from the hook next to the door and pulled it on, tugging the belt tight around her waist. She lifted Frank's fish bowl from the desk and hugged it to her body as she left. Using her old waitressing skills, she walked at a slow, steady pace, moving her legs but not her torso or arms so as to not cause a tsunami in Frank's world on the short trip to her parents' diner.

"Hang on, Frank."

Chapter Two

Allie stepped out onto the porch of her clinic, Evergreen Veterinarian Care. She glanced at Frank, then back at the blue-and-white sign behind her. She still remembered like it was yesterday the day she and Grandpa had hung that sign there. It had been a cold, snowy day just like today. Everyone else in town had been home, hunkered down that wintry night. Mom and Dad had insisted on closing the diner early so they could be a part of it, too. They'd stood out in the cold, watching until that last screw had gone into the wall. They'd applauded wildly, but Allie had barely heard them because of their gloves. It had been like watching a silent film, and she was the star.

And now she was leaving it behind. For something new. Something bigger, and different, in the city.

For a moment, she tried to imagine the bustling streets of Washington, D.C., leaving work in her lab coat—not to just walk across the street to check in with her folks. No quiet little block where she knew most everyone by name. Would strangers smile and say hello?

Her throat tightened.

Soon, someone else would take over this office and chase their dreams just like she had. She hugged Frank closer, silently wishing the new business good luck.

She locked the door behind her and carefully navigated the steps down to the street.

A fluffy snowman wearing a top hat stood next to the stairs, waving a welcoming hello to customers, and past that, three lighted wire reindeer, one with a red nose, frolicked in front of the bookstore. *Rudolph the well-read reindeer,* she amused herself. Those same decorations had been there every year since she'd been back. But she liked the way things stayed the same here in Evergreen. That was all the more reason to make the big change—to experience new things in a new town.

She looked both ways then headed across the street. Frank's water sloshed against her coat as she twisted to avoid collision with a young man hurrying past with his collar pulled high around his neck to ward off the cold wind.

At the end of Main Street, the town Christmas tree dazzled with colorful decorations. Each year, families added an ornament to the tree that became part of the collection going forward. That connection made the tree seem more personal. Not new was the giant, gold star on top, designed by the shop teacher at the local high school. How would the Evergreen Christmas tree compare to the big, fancy one at the White House?

The town had planted the Balsam Fir in front of

the gazebo about ten years ago when a farmer up on the hill, in exchange for the privilege to sell his trees there, had donated it. It hadn't been a huge tree then, but now it rose to the height of the gazebo. Before this, the town had cut and tractored a tree in each year for the holiday lighting.

Allie zipped past the post office, noticing how many people were lined up with packages to send. She was glad she didn't have anything to mail out this week. She was carrying her gift to Spencer with her on the plane—that was, if she ever got out of Evergreen.

She glanced at her watch and almost ran into one of the giant red, blue, and gold ornaments that brightened the sidewalk in front of Home Bakery. The door chimed again and again, reminding her of a Christmas handbell concert, as customers came out with bags of freshly baked goods. Business was brisk for the middle of the afternoon.

The three-foot-tall, carved nutcrackers that used to guard Grandpa's porch now stood sentry in front of Chris Kringle Kitchen—a nice addition in honor of him. All combined, it made for a cheerful sight. She never tired of Christmas in Evergreen.

She pulled the Chris Kringle Kitchen door open and stepped inside the warm diner.

"Joe! She's here." Mom rushed toward her, wearing a sweater set the color of a balsam fir, and Dad came through the green-and-white curtain that separated the kitchen from the dining area, catching up to her in long strides.

"Hi, honey." Dad wore his signature red apron, and he must have been in the middle of cooking something, because he was still carrying a red and white checkered hand towel. This restaurant had been in Dad's family for three generations, and he was the best cook she knew.

"Oh, Allie!" Carol stopped, tears spilling down her cheeks as she cocked her head as if it would be the last time they'd ever see each other. "My baby." She lunged forward, pulling Allie in for a hug.

"Mom, this is not goodbye." Allie gave her dad a pleading look as her mother clung to her neck. "I'm just dropping off Frank. Besides, you promised you wouldn't cry."

"I'm not!" Carol swept at her tears and then took the fish bowl from Allie. "I was just…chopping onions."

Dad snickered.

"I'm going to be home right after Christmas."

"Mm-hmm." Carol clung to the goldfish bowl. "And then you're leaving again right after that… for good. And all I'll have to remember you by is a goldfish."

"Maybe I should, uh…" Joe tossed the towel over his shoulder and took the goldfish bowl from Carol. "…take care of Frank, okay?"

Oh gosh, was he teary-eyed, too? Allie's heart clenched.

"Thanks, honey," Carol said to Joe.

He headed for the kitchen, and Allie placed her hands on her mother's shoulders. "Mom, Washington

D.C. has modern conveniences." Allie rubbed her shoulders, encouraging her to relax.

"I know." But Carol's words were unconvincing.

"Phone."

"I know," Carol whispered.

"I hear they even have an airport now," Allie teased.

Carol granted Allie a small smile, then took a breath. "Honey, I just want to make sure…that you're sure. Because this is a big change, Allie."

"I'm sure." She held Mom's gaze, hoping to calm her down. "It's a great job. And besides, I'm ready for a change."

Carol leveled a stare. The one Allie knew so well. "And I'm not just talking about the job."

"No. Mom." Allie raised a finger in the air, shaking her head. "No. We've been over this." She took a step back, as if the space between them would erase the comment. She was tiring of this discussion. It had been Spencer who'd found her the amazing job opportunity in Washington, D.C., and yes, he wanted her closer to him, but applying for that position had been one hundred percent her choosing. If things worked out with Spencer, that was great, but it wasn't a deal breaker. Sure, she was giving up her own vet practice here in Evergreen, but she was going to be doubling her salary in the city. There was so much opportunity in Washington, D.C. So much to see and do. It was a good change. The chance of a lifetime. "Spencer and I are just testing the waters."

"Mm-hmm. And there was a reason you two broke up, honey."

"Yeah, we couldn't handle the long-distance thing. So, now we're going to be in the same city, and…it's not a big deal," Allie said. *We'll figure it out.*

"You're going to be spending Christmas with him, Allie. That is a very big deal."

The bells on the door jingled as more customers poured in behind them, and Allie hugged Mom again.

Sniffling back tears, Mom said, "You're hugging me right now just to hush me up, aren't you?" She giggled.

"No." Her mother knew her so well. "I'm hugging you because I love you. The hushing is just a bonus." When she stepped back, she was glad to see her mom was still laughing, too.

Mom ran her fingers through Allie's hair. Her crooked smile and furrowed brow said things she didn't need to vocalize.

"I gotta go," Allie said. "I love you."

"I love you."

She kissed her mom on the cheek and headed for the door. She glanced back, watching her mom race-walk to the kitchen. She didn't have to stick around and check to know that Mom would be crying in Dad's arms in a matter of seconds. That tugged at her heart. She was tempted to run back and hug Mom one more time.

It was hard to leave, but she knew she was doing the right thing. She hoped everything would fall into place. She didn't like seeing Mom sad—especially at the holidays.

Allie reached the door, then turned and scanned the diner. So many wonderful years and memories had been made here. She'd miss this place. All the charming shelves Grandpa had built and painted white to give the diner a warm country feeling and to give Mom a spot to show off her teapot collections. The life-sized Santa sign just inside the door. The candy jar next to the register that was filled with something different every month—candy canes for December. And the snow globe.

The snow globe was a legend around here. Mom said she'd wished for a daughter on it one Christmas after she and Dad had been trying for years with no luck. Allie had been born the following September.

It wasn't to be taken lightly. Only wishes your heart truly wanted even had a chance of being granted.

Mom was nowhere in sight.

Allie dashed over to the snow globe. She lifted the glass ball from its place of honor next to the cash register and held it in her hands reverently.

Following one deep breath, she turned it upside down and gave it a good shake, then flipped it back upright, sending the snow inside twisting and swirling like a blizzard around the exact replica of the Evergreen church.

She closed her eyes and silently made her wish.

As she opened her eyes, a calm washed over her, as if there was no doubt her wish would come true. She set the snow globe down and gave it a gentle pat on the top, then headed for the door before her parents came back and saw her.

In a hurry, she almost plowed right over a sixty-something man wearing a dark suit and jaunty red scarf.

"Whoa," he said, coming to an abrupt halt.

"Oh, my gosh!" Allie exclaimed. "So sorry." She patted his arm, then, taking in his appearance—the perfectly shaped, snow-white beard and laughing eyes—she realized he was the spitting image of Santa. Come to think of it, his *Whoa!* had sounded a lot like a ho-ho-ho that a certain red-suited Christmas guy was known for. Thank goodness he hadn't fallen. That would have landed her on the naughty list for sure.

"In a hurry to get your Christmas plans started?" His blue eyes twinkled with every word, and his fluffy beard looked like the real deal. She was tempted to reach out and touch it.

"Yes." Allie couldn't believe how much this man favored jolly old St. Nicholas. It had her stumbling for words. "Just about to head out of town."

"Well…" A flash of concern crossed his face. "Be sure to check the weather before you go to the airport. Mother Nature can be unpredictable." He leaned back and gave a hearty laugh and a wink, like it was some kind of inside joke.

How did he know where she was headed? Had she said that? It didn't matter. The joke was on him. It was snowing, but that was just another wintry day in

Evergreen. No problem. She couldn't wait to set out on this journey. It was both exciting and scary to leave this place she'd called home her whole life.

The bells on the diner door jingle-jangled as the man went inside. *Would he order cookies and milk? Maybe cocoa in this weather?*

Allie smiled at the sweet man. Nice of him to offer his concern for her when she was the one who'd nearly knocked *him* over.

She walked to her truck, checking off her mental list of things to do before heading to the airport this afternoon. So far, everything was right on schedule.

Chapter Three

Allie pulled away from the curb with a heavy heart even though she was exhilarated about the journey ahead. She didn't like that Mom was so worried, but she knew she just wanted things to work out for the best. Couldn't fault her for that. *Chopping onions? Who'd buy that old excuse?*

Her house was walking distance from Main Street in good weather, but this time of year, it was better to drive and forego the risk of a broken ankle on the ice. Besides, she was on the countdown to get to the airport. She had no time to waste.

She drove around the block and pulled into the Premier Gasoline station. The owner ran out and filled up her tank. She was pretty sure she wouldn't get service in DC like she did here at the Royal Oak Garage. Not only did they give her full service on the self-serve pump, but they'd also opened the garage on the weekends or after hours when the need had arisen. And with this truck, that happened more than she liked to admit. Sometimes she wondered if the guys booby-trapped the old truck so she'd have to come in for service. They loved Grandpa's truck as much as she did.

Small-town living definitely had perks. What they lacked in volume and glitz, they made up for in fellowship and convenience. Those two businesses would probably miss her and the money they made working on her truck, too.

With her gas tank filled, she puttered around the block and headed home.

As she got within sight of her house, she thought about how it was large enough for a family of five, and she loved having that two-car garage. It made it so easy to keep all her sporting equipment, crafts, and stored holiday decorations nice and neat. She'd never realized until she'd gone hunting for a place to live in Washington, D.C. how lucky she was to have all this space. The whole apartment she'd be renting there would fit in the living room and kitchen of this house.

But how much room did a single gal really need anyway?

There was no way she could move everything she owned, so she'd planned to store some of her furniture and collections until she decided if she'd eventually buy a house there. Unfortunately, the cost of living and price of homes in DC wasn't even in the same playing field as Evergreen. Until she was more familiar with which areas were most desirable, she'd just have to rent, because the things Spencer was showing her were way out of her comfort zone—budget-wise and style-wise. Besides, she'd have the chance to meet more people living in an apartment community, and that wasn't a bad thing.

She knew every single person who lived on this street. For that matter, she knew most everyone in Evergreen. It would be fun to make new friends in a new town.

She slowed to a stop, then put her arm on the back of the seat and looked over her shoulder to back into her driveway—a necessity, since Grandpa's truck was so finicky. She never knew when she might need a jump-start. The darn thing was hit or miss, but she still loved that truck. It was her last connection to Grandpa, and they'd been so close. He was the whole reason she'd gone to North Carolina State to get her veterinarian degree. Following in his footsteps was all she'd ever wanted to do. He'd been a large animal vet, and she'd gone on calls with him from the time she was in first grade. She hoped one day she'd have someone want to walk in her shoes…or muck boots, as the case might be. Chuckling at that thought, she knew that wouldn't be the case in DC. She'd probably be wearing snappy clogs or something.

She stepped out of the truck and slammed the door behind her.

The bitter wind took her breath away. Nonetheless, she shoved her hands deep in her pockets, taking a good, long look at her home.

She'd miss this place. It had taken three rounds of painting the exterior of the Cape Cod to finally get the right shade of blue last year, and now she was leaving it behind. She'd kept the holiday decorating to a minimum since she'd be gone for the week of Christmas, but she was glad she'd taken the time to swag the pine around the porch and railings. The decorations were cheerful. She wouldn't even have a porch to decorate in her new apartment.

Oh well, less stuff to put away in January. With all Spencer seems to be planning, I'll need the extra time.

She walked carefully up the snowy sidewalk, then took the steps to the porch and unlocked the front door. Inside, stacks of labeled boxes filled part of the dining room. She'd finish packing when she got back from DC.

She set her phone and purse down, then got her suitcase and tote bag from her bedroom and wheeled them into the dining room. She did a quick dash through the house, unplugging things and checking for forgotten items.

Her cell phone rang. She ran to grab it from where she'd set it down on the old sideboard she'd refinished. The Christmas cards she'd received reflected back from the beveled 1900's mirror. She recognized the number on the caller ID immediately.

"Spencer," she said. "Hey, I was just heading out the door."

"Happy 'moving to DC day'!"

"Hey, it's not 'moving to DC day'," Allie reminded him. "It's 'coming to DC to sign the lease on my apartment day'."

"I'm sorry, do they make a card for that?" Spencer teased.

"They make a card for everything." She grabbed her new rolling suitcase, slid her carryon bag over the handle, and headed for the door as they talked.

"I can't believe we're going to be living in the same city together. Five blocks apart."

"Well, the commute will definitely be a lot easier." Allie lifted her suitcase and went down the front steps, then rolled it to the truck.

"So, I've got some incredible stuff lined up for us. Dinners, parties, oh, and on Christmas Day, you and I will be going to my boss's swanky estate in the Hamptons," Spencer said. "One of the partners even said that we can use his helicopter to get there!"

"A helicopter?" She swung her carry-on into the back of the truck. *Who flies around in a helicopter?* And was she seriously traveling all the way from Vermont to DC only to end up halfway back home in The Hamptons? "Really..." She pushed the handle down on the suitcase, then heaved it over the wooden rails into the truck bed, too.

"Better get used to it, okay? This is going to be a brand-new start for us, Allie."

And a huge change for me. I don't mind a little slow, quiet time for reflection now and then. "Right. And I'm excited about that." Her mom's concerns echoed in her mind. "I just want to make sure that we're not getting ahead of ourselves."

"Allie. I get it. I totally get it, okay? I just want to

put the last couple of months behind us. I mean, this is Christmas. The time for new beginnings."

"Absolutely. And you know, also... I love swanky parties." She hoped he bought that. She'd never even been to one. She climbed into the driver's seat of her significantly less-than-swanky '56 Ford pickup truck and slammed the door. She'd been to Spencer's office before. Now that was swanky. She pictured him sitting at his desk the day she'd met him there for lunch. The lunch he'd ended up not being able to go to. Instead, he'd ordered fancy French food for them to enjoy while he'd talked on a conference call. She'd have rather gotten a hot dog from the cart downstairs, but he'd been pretty pleased with himself for coming up with that contingency plan when the unscheduled meeting had popped up on his calendar.

He worked out of a corner office with heavy, dark wooden furniture and plush leather couches, nicer than a lot of people would have in their house. The view was amazing: the whole skyline of D.C., with the Washington Monument towering right in the center of it all. Spencer's crocodile leather chair was probably what she remembered most. She'd never seen anything like it, and who knew crocodile leather could be so soft? He'd let her sit in it, and it had been so cushy she hadn't wanted to get back up. She'd wished for crocodile boots ever since.

That visit should have given her a hint at the highfalutin future they'd have together, but now, with her moving there, things were beginning to get real.

"Beautiful," Spencer said. "I should get back to work, though. I can't wait to see you tonight."

"All right. I'll talk to you soon. Bye." She disconnected the call. Her truck was decorated in garland with wreaths on the grill and tailgate. It had been the first truck Grandpa had ever bought for himself. He'd had many others over the years but had never let this one go. It had been so special to him, and because of that, it was extra special to her. Special. Not swanky. It would be out of place on the busy streets of Washington, D.C. But that could be a good thing. Not too many people had a truck like this. It would be a conversation starter.

Allie sat taller in the seat. "I can do swanky." She put her phone down and imagined her new life in DC. She had shopping to do. Swanky was hardly how'd she describe even the dressiest outfit she'd packed.

Ready to get this adventure started, she cranked her truck. It whirred and groaned, but didn't fire up. She dropped her head to the steering wheel. *Not again.*

Chapter Four

Ryan Bellamy was thankful his in-laws were still so involved in his daughter's life. He was lucky they only lived a couple of hours away. Telling them about the change in plans for Christmas this year had made him nervous, but he couldn't bear another Christmas like last year.

He was determined to make this one as opposite as possible from that.

His in-laws had been understanding about him wanting to take Zoe away, rearranging their schedule to spend time with her at the beginning of her school break instead of on Christmas Day, as had been tradition since Zoe was just a baby.

It was hard for them all, going through Christmas without Sarah.

The two-hour drive to pick up Zoe had made him melancholy. The house had seemed so quiet without Zoe around the last few days.

The thirty-minute ferry ride flew by. He'd

daydreamed it away in what seemed like only a moment. He jogged to his car and waited to disembark.

Once he got back on the road, he returned calls, using the Bluetooth so he could keep both hands on the wheel. It had too noisy with the wind to do that on the ferry. He glanced at the speedometer on the rental car. He'd set the cruise control, but these small towns' speed limits going up and down always kept him on his toes.

Finally, he made it to his in-laws' house. Panic swept through him as memories from past Christmases ascended on him.

He hadn't even taken his key from the ignition when Zoe bounded out of the house, running toward him. She'd missed him, too. He jumped out of the car, picked her up, and swung her around. Zoe made his heart complete. He shared quick thank-yous and goodbyes with his in-laws, then got right back on the road.

He skipped the ferry and went the long way around. This Christmas would be like no other, starting right now. No ferry ride.

That was the plan, and he'd make one hundred percent certain he succeeded. Zoe deserved a happy holiday, and he was going to be sure she got it.

The roads were clear as they drove through the Vermont woods. Snow covered everything else around them. The trees bowed from the weight on their branches, and every once in a while, a pile of snow fell like a mini-avalanche.

Zoe sat quietly in the backseat. He was happy to have her within arms' reach again.

His phone rang, and he took the call. No matter how much he planned for time off, he always ended up slammed with calls the whole first day he tried to get out of town. Not a single call he'd returned earlier that day had been urgent, and he had a doctor covering for him for anything that was.

He heard a quiet sigh from the backseat. She had to be getting bored.

Maybe he'd have been better off letting Zoe field his calls like she'd offered. She seemed to be eight going on twenty-eight most days. Then again, losing a parent at her age had a way of making a kid grow up faster than they should have to.

More often than not, Zoe handled his wife's passing better than him.

"I gotta go," Ryan said into the phone. This wasn't how he'd planned to start this trip. He'd pictured this ride full of laughter and Christmas carols. Time to fix that. "Christmas calls. Bye." He pressed the button on his Bluetooth to hang up. "Sorry." He made eye contact with Zoe in the rearview mirror. "Last work call." He laughed, trying to be playful. "I promise."

"You said that after the last one," Zoe reminded him.

Busted. He had said that.

"And the one before that, and the one before that."

"Whoa. Okay." He sighed. She was right. He was terrible at unplugging from work. "Hey, Zoe. *Now* I'm officially on vacation. Just you and me off to Florida and our big cruise on Christmas Day. Won't that be fun?"

"Sure. We can have fun in Florida," Zoe said, but he could tell she wasn't completely sold on the idea yet. "I mean, Christmas is supposed to be cold with snow, but…"

But? "According to who?"

"Santa!" Zoe looked at him matter-of-factly. "That's why he wears a suit."

A mental picture of Santa in a pair of red-and-white, furry beach britches made him chuckle. "Aaah. You know, I didn't know that." Ryan wasn't too worried about Zoe's lack of excitement about the trip to Florida. He was sure she'd have fun once they got there.

It was hard breaking tradition, but there was no way he was going to allow those old family memories to haunt them the way they had last year. That was just too hard. His heart couldn't bear wallowing in that sad place again this year. But worse than the heartbreak of losing Sarah had been seeing Zoe struggle with that loss. They'd been so close, always working on projects together. They'd even had matching outfits and had gone for mother-daughter spa days.

Those were voids he'd never be able to fill. Anything he could do to make things better, he'd do, and being as far away from a traditional Christmas as he could possibly get was the plan for this year.

He regretted being on the phone for part of the ride so far. He hadn't meant for that to happen. He'd do better. No more calls, and his New Year's resolution was going to be to find better life balance to score more quality time with Zoe. They needed to start building new, good memories of their own together.

"But how about this?" Ryan reasoned with her. "Tell you what. When we get there, as soon as we get into our hotel, we will crank up the air conditioning really high, and we'll fill the pool with ice, and it'll be just like living in the North Pole."

Zoe rolled her eyes, looking at him like he'd flat-out lost his mind, but at least she was laughing. "Oh, Dad."

Okay, so it was doubtful the resort would let him turn one of their swimming pools into an artic adventure, but it was the thought that counted. Right?

On the bright side, they had a few days to enjoy Florida before the cruise left port. They'd do some warm weather shopping and visit a couple of attractions. As much as she loved animals, he was pretty sure she'd flip over seeing dolphins, whales, and sea lions up close. Truth be told, he was pretty excited about it, too. When the ship docked in Grand Cayman, they were booked for the Turtle Farm excursion, where they'd get to handle the turtles and even swim with them in the lagoon.

If all went according to plan, Zoe would be asking Santa for another sunny Christmas vacation next year.

Chapter Five

It was moments like this that Allie, for just a nanosecond, wished she hadn't sold her reliable Ford Excursion when Grandpa had died and left her his truck. It had been his pride and joy; then again, he'd been an ace mechanic. He'd done the full body-off restoration on it over a two-year period. It was factory down to the rivets, as he'd liked to say. He could work on anything from kitchen appliances to tractors, and he'd taught her plenty over the years. She wished now she'd paid even closer attention. On a bright note, she'd gotten pretty good at doctoring up the old truck to get it going again.

She walked around to the front of the truck, pushed the wreath that hung from the hood ornament to the side, and jimmied the latch on the hood, coaxing it to release.

It squeaked as she raised it. She reached over the shiny radiator, down inside the engine compartment toward the distributor cap, and got to work. It would've been a lot easier if she'd been a couple of inches taller.

She lifted one leg off the ground, stretching to give the wires a good jiggle and checking for anything loose. Her road calls took her down rough country lanes sometimes. She assumed that was why sometimes, just a simple wiggle made all the difference.

"You could've walked to DC by now."

Allie almost bumped her head on the hood twisting toward Michelle Lansing. She'd recognize her voice anywhere. She extricated herself from the truck and turned to see Michelle marching toward her, carrying a box wrapped in blue Christmas paper that almost matched her coat. It was filled with a half dozen giant, glittery Styrofoam snowflakes.

"Don't we have enough *real* snow?"

"Oh, this is for the Christmas festival." Michelle lifted the box to make her point. Her brown curls bounced with each word. Glitter sparkled on the lapel of her coat. "You know, the one you're going to miss?"

"Yes, I'm aware I'll be missing the Christmas festival. Thank you for the reminder." Allie made one last tweak under the hood.

"I'll tell you, whoever decided to take over after you planned this thing is crazy."

Allie snickered as she twisted to see her friend. "You're taking over the planning!" She'd talked Michelle into it when she'd decided to make the big move to DC.

"Like I said…"

Allie got a good laugh out of that. She'd loved planning the festival. Yes, it was a lot of work, but everyone in town looked forward to it all throughout the year. It had been a labor of love for her, but she'd been doing it for so long, it really didn't seem all that complicated anymore. Not so unlike making your first Thanksgiving dinner for a crowd. It was scary as heck, but after a few years, you knew exactly what order to cook things in so everything was done at the same time, and it seemed like a breeze. Michelle would have it down pat soon, too.

She slammed the hood and turned to Michelle as she brushed her hands together to get the grease from her fingers.

"Oh, boy. Don't tell me you're taking this thing to DC."

"Of course I am," Allie said. "This was my grandpa's truck." She gave the rounded curves a loving pat. "I love this truck."

"Well, it obviously doesn't love you."

"Why are we friends again?" Allie teased.

"Because I'm the only one who will tell you that you are *never* going to get this thing to start."

Allie straightened the live wreath that hung from the hood. "Oh, yeah? Watch this." She gave Michelle a cocky nod, then crossed her fingers it would start. Holding her breath, she dropped into the driver's seat and turned the key. Without a moment's hesitation, the truck started right up. "See. It worked!" She was as surprised as Michelle was, but she'd never admit it.

"Great!" Michelle trudged through the yard,

leaving a path in the snow all the way to the truck. "Now you can take me to town hall."

"No. I have to get to the airport," she said.

"It's on the way!" Michelle put the box of snowflakes on the middle of the bench seat. "And this box is awkward. So let's go." She slid in and pulled the door closed.

Allie stared at her friend. This was exactly the reason Michelle was the right person to take over the duties of the Christmas Festival. She was bossy and determined.

If town hall weren't on the way, she'd make her get out of her truck right now. But Michelle had a point. It was just a few blocks down the road. In a town the size of Evergreen, there wasn't much that wasn't along the route.

One way in. One way out.

She still couldn't get used to the remodeled town hall building. Once an all-red brick building that used to be the school, it was now sided in a soft dove gray lapboard with white trim, accented with cranberry-colored doors. It had been a great improvement; it was just strange to see the light-colored building in this spot.

This year's Christmas Festival banner had already been hung high above the doors. Never an easy task. She was delighted that they'd kept the same design she'd created long ago. The tri-colored, weather-resistant banner had snowy-white Christmas trees in each corner and a green ribbon across the bottom with a bow right in the middle, like a perfectly wrapped

Christmas present. Above the bow read *48th Annual Evergreen Christmas Festival.* A matching banner would be hung in front of the gazebo on Main Street soon, where many of the outdoor gatherings would happen.

People carried tall boxes as they headed inside— probably more trees to decorate. Two men hung over a ladder, trying to finish stringing lights in the huge shrubbery in front.

On the steep stairs to the front doors on the second floor, the six-foot-tall nutcrackers dressed in all of their Christmas finery guarded the entryway. Allie had always struggled with where to put those huge nutcrackers. And there were seven of them to place. A gift from a well-loved resident long ago, they had to be as old as she was, and they were heavy. But they were tradition, so they were part of the equation, even though not a year went by that the ominous statues didn't send at least one tiny tot crying into the arms of his parents.

Allie stopped in front of the building and waited for Michelle to get out of the truck.

"You've got to come in," her friend pleaded.

"I've got to go."

"But I want you to see the layout. We're changing some things. Come on."

She could spare a couple of minutes for her friend. It was important to her. Besides, Allie was curious. "Okay. One minute." Allie knew how hard Michelle had been working on this project. She left the truck running rather than risk it not starting again. "You've got one minute." She hopped out and jogged to catch up with Michelle, who'd raced ahead, carrying the fake snowflakes and dodging two guys clearing snow from the walkway.

They ran up the steps side-by-side, then Michelle backed up to the door and pushed it open, letting Allie go in first.

The inside of town hall buzzed with activity. Teams of people decorated Christmas trees with shiny plastic balls in festive colors. Another group strung giant snowflakes, like the ones Michelle was carrying, from the rafters and on nails along the walls. It was all hands on deck to prepare for the festival. The whole building smelled of fresh pine from the trees. Lights and decorations put the dazzle on the greenery like a sparkling jeweled necklace, making the finishing touches on a beautiful gown.

"This looks amazing!" Allie stepped inside and twirled, trying to take it all in. What Michelle had already completed in such a short time was impressive. Long tables served as workstations around the room, and folks seemed to be enjoying themselves. There was no shortage of volunteers. Michelle handed off the box of fake snowflakes to one of them.

"You did such a good job," Allie said.

Her friend pulled her hands to her heart. "Thank you."

Allie noticed the new mayor, Ezra Green, giving orders to one of the snowflake makers. "This one needs a little more sparkle…" he said, handing it back to her.

What does he know?

Ezra's father had been mayor all the years Allie had run the festival, and Ezra and his dad were as different as night and day. Mayor Green, Sr. had always stayed out of the way, simply reminding her once in a while to keep up the traditions and trusting her to get the job done. He was laid back, never in a hurry, and always wore a smile. Ezra was up to his elbows in the middle of things, plus he had an abundance of nervous energy that was unsettling—like a piece of live wire dancing around. That would've driven her crazy.

Michelle's shoulders drooped. "Uh-oh. Here comes the mayor. I haven't had enough coffee for this."

Allie couldn't get used to referring to Ezra, who she'd known since grade school, as mayor. "There's not enough coffee in Evergreen," she agreed.

Ezra marched over to them. "Michelle, I have an idea." As jittery as a Chihuahua in a room full of strangers, he could hardly stand still.

"Good morning, Ezra," Allie said.

He all but growled in her direction. "Former resident."

"I haven't even left yet!" He'd taken her decision to relocate so personally.

Michelle gave him half a chance. "What's your idea this time, Ezra?"

"I think we should have an app," he announced, way too proud of himself, standing there with his big idea as bold as brass. "You know, an interactive experience."

"The festival is in five days. We can't get an app made in five days." Michelle's frustration level rose.

Clearly, this wasn't the first harebrained, last-minute idea the new mayor had tossed her way. Allie was so glad she'd never had to deal with Ezra when she'd been planning the festival.

His eyes bugged out like he was about to explode. "Well, we need to find some way to make the festival current. We need to shake things up." He did a little shimmy shake that made her think of the chicken dance. If only she had that much energy.

Michelle brushed her curls from her face, a nervous habit from way back. "This is my first year in charge, and I don't want to shake things up."

Ezra narrowed his eyes. "It's my first year as mayor, and I *want* things shaken."

Michelle sucked in a breath, and then let him have it. "Your dad was mayor for thirty years, and this was good enough for him."

It was taking all Allie had to stand there and hold her tongue.

"That's my point!" Ezra said. "We don't want this to be our parents' festival."

Michelle turned to Allie for help. "Allie?"

"Don't look at me." She threw her hands up. "Soon-to-be former resident, remember?"

Ezra wiggled his brows in a way that was as annoying as a kid brother, although Allie was pretty sure that wasn't what he was going for.

"Hey, everyone. I came to help out."

Allie spun around to see the newest addition to Evergreen heading their way. Barbara Rousseau, once an executive at one of the largest financial institutions in the nation, had bought the big turn-of-the-century home at the corner of Green Street and Pine Drive. Years ago, it had been a bed and breakfast, but it had gone into foreclosure and sat empty for years, falling into disrepair. Finally, a distant family member had put it on the market. The place had needed some serious TLC, but the widow had taken an early retirement and invested her money and her vision into the place, and it hadn't taken her long to transform it. Folks anxiously awaited her grand opening on Valentine's Day, but recent rumors had it that she'd be opening at the first of the year.

The pretty redhead was all bundled up against the weather in a camel-colored coat and colorful infinity scarf, more corporate than small-town Evergreen.

"Barbara! How's the inn coming?" Allie asked.

Her face lit up. "Oh, my goodness. So great! We're opening in two weeks. I can't believe it."

So, rumors were true. That was great news, because there wasn't an inn or hotel within miles of Evergreen. Until now. Nice lodging in the area would help everyone.

Ezra did that weird brow wiggle again. "It's so nice to have someone move to Evergreen to open a business."

"Thanks," Barbara said.

He turned his gaze to Allie. "Instead of business owners moving away."

"Okay, meanie," she said to Ezra. "Don't make me tell them about the incident in second grade."

Ezra paused, then pasted a smile on his face and said, "Best of luck in your new job."

Allie and the girls exchanged a knowing glance. She'd put Ezra right in his place. Honestly, she wasn't sure which thing he was so worried about her telling; there were so many. It could've been anything from the time he'd cut her left pigtail off at the shoulder when he'd sat behind her, to the time the teacher had asked him to "tell her more" and he'd broken out in the song from *Grease*, to the time he'd told everyone that his ancestors had come over on the cauliflower. He'd always been a funny kid with way too much energy, but he'd also been one of the brightest. As irritating as he could be, it was true that he'd probably do great things for Evergreen.

"Michelle"—Ezra was clearly eager to change the subject—"since Doc Hadley retired and moved away, we need someone new to play Santa. I'm thinking we go against type: younger, handsome..." He stroked his hair, preening, in hopes for their approval.

Michelle shut him down. "Too late. I already got a guy out of Burlington."

"I think I saw him," Allie said. "He looks like Santa Claus even without the costume."

"Wait? He's here already?" Michelle was surprised. "Must be getting ready for the role."

"Well, okay. If you want to be traditional," Ezra said. "But what about the children's choir? Can't they do some newer Christmas songs?"

The only somewhat-newer Christmas song Allie could think of off the top of her head was "Grandma Got Run Over By A Reindeer," and she wasn't so sure that was a good choice for the family event.

Michelle shook her head, but Allie was pretty sure her friend would like to shake Ezra right about now. "Give me a break." Michelle threw up her hands and walked away.

Barbara and Allie tried to hold back their snickers as Ezra ran after Michelle, begging her to listen to more of his great ideas.

Chapter Six

As Ryan drove through scenic Vermont, the mountains towered above them on either side. Blanketed in snow, the evergreens rose, green with their branches dragging. The snow was coming down good. Blowing in big, blurry gusts in front of him. He was glad they were traveling during the day. This would be treacherous at night.

"Silent Night" filled the car while he and Zoe played their favorite car trip game.

"Okay," he said, wondering why after playing this game with her for so many years that he didn't have a list of words memorized already. His letter was F. *What Christmas word starts with an F?* "We've got... Angels, Blitzen, Candy Canes, Decorations, Elves... Fireplace!"

He glanced at Zoe in his rearview mirror. She cocked her head. "Fireplace isn't a Christmas word."

"It's what Santa comes down."

"Santa comes down the *chimney*." Zoe wasn't as easily convinced now as she had been at five or six.

Maybe it was just as well he didn't remember the words he'd gotten away with back then.

"Okay. Okay. Umm. How about...fruitcake." Ryan glanced in the rearview mirror to see her reaction.

"Pretty good," Zoe admitted.

"Pretty good?"

"Okay," she said with a giggle. "My turn. G."

"Okay," Ryan urged her.

"Angels, Blitzen, Candy Canes, Decorations, Elves, Fruitcake, and...Gingerbread." Zoe smiled with that toothy grin he loved so much. It would no doubt set him back thousands of dollars in orthodontics not too far down the road, but for now, he adored that smile just the way it was.

"Mmm. Mm. Mm," Zoe said, clearly proud of the answer she'd come up with.

"That's a good one."

"Thanks. Except...now I'm hungry," she said, hugging her tummy.

"Okay. You know what?" He glanced at the clock on the dash. "I think we have time to stop. We just have to make it quick. We've got a flight to catch."

A couple of minutes later, Zoe pointed out a sign. "Evergreen! Let's go there."

"Yeah, sure." It was on the way. Who was he to argue? They'd grab a bite, top off the fuel, and be on their way. "Sounds good." He slowed down and took the exit toward Evergreen.

The speed limit was only thirty-five miles per hour. After being on the interstate for a while, it felt like they were creeping down the rural route. He was beginning to worry the town might be too far off the interstate and they might have to turn around, when he came upon a big green sign on the side of the road with an arrow to turn.

The sign read *Welcome to Evergreen* and was decorated with a red-and-white picture of a jolly Santa Claus holding a candy cane above the town name.

"We're here, Dad!"

They took the turn and drove through a red covered bridge that crossed over the semi-frozen creek they'd been driving alongside for miles.

Ryan was kind of surprised he and Sarah had never happened across Evergreen. When he'd first started practicing medicine and times had been lean, they'd taken day trips in the car. They'd been to nearly every covered bridge in the area. How had they missed this one? There were plenty of them in this region, each unique and special in its own way. Somewhere, there was a scrapbook with pictures Sarah had taken on all of those trips.

"It's so pretty," Zoe said.

They drove out the other side of the bridge, and almost magically, the landscape opened up, revealing all the buildings and the town below in the valley. A pretty white church sat on the edge of town, its tall steeple reaching to the sky.

It looked storybook perfect.

Allie left town hall and drove over to Main Street, pulling into an empty parking spot in front of the post office across from her clinic.

She'd worked so hard to open her veterinary practice in Evergreen. It had been her dream for so long. She'd done well, experiencing steady growth every year, but it was time to find her place in this big world. The job in DC was an awesome opportunity. She wouldn't be handling large animals anymore; that group only handled domestic pets—cats and dogs— and a few exotics. No house calls, either.

Being a vet in a big city practice was going to be quite a switch. No longer would she have to keep her medical bag at the ready for any emergency that might arise day or night. Her truck wouldn't be a second medical closet, and her wardrobe wouldn't consist of muck boots and a heavy coat anymore. Not that she'd ever minded that.

She picked up the FOR SALE sign from the seat next to her and got out of the truck. She walked across the street and hung it on the front of her building. She let out a long breath. Moving was feeling very real now. She placed a loving hand on the wooden frame that held her sign against the wall.

EVERGREEN VETERINARIAN CARE
Allie Shaw
Doctor of Veterinarian Medicine

Would another vet move in? That would be nice for her patients, but most likely, that wouldn't happen.

The only local student who'd gone to veterinarian school had decided to study abroad in England, and she hadn't come back.

In two months, this spot might be a nail salon, or yarn store. Although, she knew the town needed a dentist. Everyone had to travel at least forty miles for dental care. They were getting more and more artists moving to Evergreen. Maybe one of them would take the leap of faith and open a shop here.

With the B&B opening, they might actually start getting enough overnight tourist traffic to help support something like that.

The small storefront had been her first big purchase in Evergreen. She'd decided to take her parents up on the offer to live with them for a year to be able to buy it, putting her house hunting on hold after she'd come back from college. It had been a wise decision.

It wasn't likely anyone would inquire about the sale of the office space over the Christmas holiday, but it was time to start nailing down the final items on her checklist. This was one less thing to worry about when she got home.

She stood on the porch, looking down Main Street, as she had done countless times in the past. There were so many memories here. The snow swirled around her, adding a festive sheen to the town and an extra glisten to the garland around every doorframe and window. Street signs and lampposts were done up in red and white ribbons, like giant candy cane treats. Christmas was her favorite time of the year in Evergreen, and this would be the first one she'd ever spent away. Even in her college days, when others went skiing or stayed back at the dorm, she'd always made the trip home. Was she homesick already? She hadn't even left yet, and she already had that empty feeling in the pit of her stomach.

DC will be pretty, too, she reminded herself.

Ready to start her adventure, she crossed the street to where she'd parked between her parents' diner and the post office. "Merry Christmas!" she called out to a neighbor coming out of the bakery. Her phone rang just as she reached her truck and she answered it. "Hey, Henry." He spoke quickly, sounding panicked, and all she could make out was the word "Buttercup." "What's wrong?"

"Doc. Buttercup is in labor. You have to come quick."

"Oh, no. No. No. She's not due for—"

"You've got to come. Something's wrong," he pleaded.

"Oh, no. Henry, I'm on my way to the airport. Can't you call Dr. Myers?"

"I did. He's over in Montpelier on another emergency."

A pang of anxiety hit her. "Oh." She couldn't leave Henry in a lurch. If something happened to that cow, she'd never forgive herself.

"He'll never make it in time," Henry explained. "Plus, you know Buttercup. Please. You've got to come."

She checked her watch. She didn't have much

time. She still needed to stop and say goodbye to her parents, make the drive over to the airport, and get checked in for her flight. Who knew how long the security line would be this afternoon? But Henry had been one of her customers since day one. "Right. Okay. I'll be there as soon as I can."

"Thank you, Doc. Thank you."

"Bye." She hung up the phone.

She couldn't leave town in good conscience with Henry so upset—understandably so. He'd dumped a fortune in transferring prizewinning Holstein embryos into his old Jersey cows to carry them. He'd spent every last bit of the inheritance from his father on a huge new barn, which he hadn't even put a pitchfork in yet, and those cows. His whole herd was counting on this upgrade.

"Oh, man." She let go of a heavy sigh as she got into the truck.

She was in a hurry, but when she turned the key, it was clear that her truck wasn't. Grandpa's old '56 Ford was as unpredictable as the Vermont weather in the springtime.

The truck chug-chug-chugged and cranked, but didn't start...again. Looking to heaven, she said, "Seriously? I know you don't want me to leave, but this is getting ridiculous." She'd never get to the airport at this rate.

She waited a minute, pressing the gas pedal twice— once because it needed it, and once for good luck. It worked most of the time. She cranked the truck again, but it choked and stuttered like a dying rooster.

She gave it another try, leaning into the steering wheel like that would help, when a knock on her passenger window startled her. She reached over, stretching to crank the window down. "Hi there?" She didn't recognize the man or the little girl.

"Hi. Do you need some help?" the man in the lightweight dress coat asked. He was handsome, with sandy brown hair and blue eyes. The little girl was bundled up in a gray coat with a fur-edged hood. She climbed up on the running board and leaned in the window with a grin.

"Oh, no," Allie said, trying to act nonchalant. "It'll start." She shrugged like it was no big deal. "Eventually." Embarrassment rose in her cheeks. She hoped he hadn't noticed. This wouldn't normally faze her. All it took was a little patience, but today, she was in a hurry.

The man crossed his fingers. "Wishing you luck."

She gave him a "thank you" smile. Frustrated, she twisted the key one more time. The truck started. "Oh!" She snapped her head toward him in surprise, and her jaw dropped. "Hey!" *How lucky was that?*

They shared a look of surprise.

The little girl was beaming, her eyes wide. "Did you do that, Dad?"

"You know, when I tell the story later, I fully intend to take credit for it, so yes. Let's say I did."

The little girl giggled, pushing her long brown hair over her shoulders.

Allie loved the banter between father and daughter. "How can I ever thank both of you?"

"You could direct us to a good place for lunch."

"The Chris Kringle Kitchen is right here. It's the best diner in town, and I'm not just saying that because my folks run it."

He leaned further into the window. "Chris Kringle? Kitchen? My goodness. You guys really take Christmas seriously around here, don't you?"

"Yes, we sure do. Thanks a lot for your help. Couldn't have done it without you," Allie said.

"Absolutely." Their eyes connected for a long moment, then he stepped away from the truck. She liked the way his eyes crinkled when he smiled. A real smile.

"Merry Christmas." The young girl waved as she climbed down from the running board.

Allie heart filled with joy from the little girl's Christmas wish. "Merry Christmas." *That was so sweet of them to stop.*

She watched them walk down the sidewalk hand-in-hand. Through the open window, Allie heard the girl say, "See, Dad? This is what Christmas is *supposed* to look like."

He answered her with, "Florida will look like Christmas, too. Only with palm trees."

Allie laughed out loud. She was pretty sure the girl wasn't going to buy that. Everyone knew Christmas was supposed to be snowy. Florida? Palm trees? No way.

She piloted her truck away from the curb, passing them just as they walked into Chris Kringle Kitchen. She should've told them to try the fish and chips. Dad made the best around.

At the stop sign, she noticed the Christmas Festival team had also hung the festival sign over the gazebo. She wished she'd told the strangers there'd be carolers there later this afternoon. That was always a fun part of the day. She hoped they didn't miss it. Mom would probably mention it to them. She was great about things like that.

They're going to love Evergreen. Too bad they're just passing through. They seem nice.

Chapter Seven

Allie drove to the outskirts of town to Henry's farm. The sprawling acreage had been handed down over four generations of Holloways, and now Henry was grooming his boys to take over.

Her tires crunched in the icy snow as she followed the ruts, like a train on rails, along the snow-covered dirt lane that led back to the barn. A couple of Henry's goats had wandered off again, playing king of the mountain on a snowdrift.

Her truck slid a little as she steered into the curve. At least if she got stuck in the snow here, Henry had plenty of equipment to get her out and on the road again.

The two goats abandoned their game and began running and jumping alongside the truck as if they'd crowned themselves the welcoming committee. She hit her brakes, afraid she'd run over them. Crazy goats.

The turn-of-the-century farmhouse sat up on the hill to the right, but this lane led to the equipment sheds, an old wooden-and-concrete dairy barn and the one that had just been built. The new barn only highlighted how faded the old red barn was, making it appear almost a muddy pink in comparison.

Henry stood outside of the old barn, talking to one of his boys. A lazy rooster with long, dark red, sickle-like tail feathers pecked his way through the snow alongside Henry.

Allie tooted the horn and leaned out her truck window. "Hey, Henry." She pulled to a stop near the red gate at the old barn and rolled up her window.

Henry walked over to the truck as she got out. "Hey, Doc." His face was etched with worry. He pushed his gloved hands into the pockets of his heavy canvas coat.

She changed into a pair of muck boots, gathered her work coat and her medicine bag from the back of the truck, and followed Henry.

The old barn smelled of good hay and the essence of livestock that always made her relax. A city girl would be pinching her nose right now. She shuffle-ball-changed around a few scattered chickens and walked past all of the stalls with horses, to the very end where Buttercup was spending her last few weeks before calving.

Henry must've been taking his role as grandfather pretty seriously these days, because this was the first time she'd ever seen his barn with white twinkle lights running along every stall down the aisle. It looked festive.

She took off her good coat and laid it over the top of the wooden stall door, then pulled on her green, waterproof work jacket that covered most of her outfit. Then she stepped into the stall with Buttercup.

She rubbed the cow's head, said a few comforting words, and then examined her. Henry stood nearby, watching as nervous as if it were his first child.

"Sorry, Henry," she said, stepping back. "She's not in labor." She still didn't have the spring Allie would expect right before calving, and although she was doing a good amount of mooing, those weren't attached to contractions.

Henry stood with his arm propped on the stall gate. "Are you sure? I heard her mooing."

"Cows moo, Henry," she teased. "It's a fairly common occurrence." For a seasoned horseman, he sure was frantic about these cows. If she didn't know better, she'd have thought he'd never been around livestock at all, but there was a rack of ribbons and trophies for his horses that covered the back wall of three stalls. His dad had always handled the cattle. This was all new for Henry.

He shook his head. "It was a different kind. It was an I'm-about-to-give-birth moo."

"You'd better brush up on your bovine, because she's fine." Maybe she should create an app for that. Bovine translator. Sounded like something Ezra would get behind. She chuckled to herself as she took off her gloves.

"What are we going to do if it happens when you're gone?"

So, that was what this was about. It was a nice compliment that folks preferred her over the neighboring town's veterinarian, but it sure was exhausting with everyone hurrying to get everything they needed done before she left town for good. And when it came to Buttercup, you just couldn't rush these kinds of things.

If she'd said it once, she'd said it a hundred times. "Call Dr. Myers in Montpelier." She unzipped her work jacket. "I have a plane to catch."

Henry grabbed her red wool dress coat from the stall and ran after her with it. "Here." He took her work jacket from her and held her coat up for her to slip into.

"Thank you." She picked up her medical bag and headed for the truck.

Henry mumbled, "That big-city living is going to change you."

"Oh, stop. Change isn't a bad thing." She pointed to the brand-new barn that sat only forty feet from the old one. "Look at that. You built a new barn. That's not a bad thing." That barn had to have cost Henry over a hundred grand. It was one of those fancy metal jobs with sliding doors at both ends tall enough for him to drive his big equipment through if he wanted. He'd told her this barn would hold over 2,400 square bales in the loft alone. A plus, since his boys had purchased the neighboring acreage last summer and started baling squares and round bales for their own farm use and retail. That barn opened up new opportunities for Henry and the next generation of Holloway men.

"Haven't moved into it yet, and it's just a barn," Henry said.

She knew better than that. It was way more than *just* a barn to him. "And I will still be Allie. Just in a new city." She turned to face him. "What are you going to do with the old barn once you move in?"

"Dunno. Tear it down, probably."

"Ahhh. See that, Henry?" She placed her bag in the truck. "More change. It's in the air. You can feel it." She patted him on the chest. "Merry Christmas, Henry." She climbed into the driver's seat.

"Merry Christmas, Doc." He closed the door for her but waited.

Allie was pretty sure he was hanging close in case she needed help. Last time she was here, he'd had to bring the tractor around and give her a jump-start.

She hoped for the best as she turned the key, but there was no problem this time. The engine started right up. She and Henry both let out a whoop.

"There we go!" Thank goodness her truck was finally cooperating. She had places to go. A journey to begin.

"Bye." Henry turned his back to the wind and headed to the barn.

She waved and pulled away as those two white goats followed along close behind her. They'd probably been nibbling on the wreath on the back of her truck. An occupational hazard.

She loved her patients—the furry ones and their guardians.

Now, to get ready to leave for the airport.

Chapter Eight

Ryan and Zoe stepped inside the Chris Kringle Kitchen.

This place sure lives up to its name. Ryan half expected there to be a giant chair at one end of the diner with kids in line for the chance to tell Santa their last-minute adjustments to their Christmas lists.

A pretty woman with shoulder-length blond hair wearing a green sweater set greeted them. "Just the two of you this afternoon?"

"Yes."

"Follow me." She led them to a table across the room. He couldn't glance in any direction without getting an eyeful of red and green—from the curtains to the napkins and even the dishes on display.

The windows were frosted with fake snow that appeared to be year-round decor. Didn't they have plenty of real snow right now?

He thought about the woman in her bright red, vintage truck.

Not only did this town take Christmas seriously,

but she did, too. She had a wreath on the shiny front grille of that antique, and another one on the back, nearly covering the entire tailgate end-to-end. It was a very nice truck. Not the kind you expected to see someone driving around town on a snowy day.

He had no idea why he'd even stopped and asked if he could help. Changing a flat tire was about the extent of his car knowledge, and he wasn't local, so he had no connections in this town to assist her.

Ryan chalked it up to holiday spirit. Who knew crossing your fingers could start a truck? Kind of a superhero power. He liked the way her nose had wrinkled when she'd laughed. Fresh and funny. Very much the girl next door.

He hadn't even caught her name. All he knew was that her parents owned this place.

He wondered if the woman seating them was her mother. She had a nice smile, too.

Why was it the chance encounter with someone nice had to be somewhere he'd never be again? He could use good company like her.

The place was packed. It appeared he and Zoe had snagged the very last table.

For a diner, it had a nice holiday vibe. Every table was draped with a red cloth and a gold table runner. Red and gold bows snazzed up the back of every wooden chair. Paper napkins in a festive gold-and-white pattern made the place seem homey. This wasn't an average greasy spoon. Twinkle lights not only brightened the huge Christmas tree in the corner, but also lined the whole path across the refrigerated glass-front case filled with goodies.

He opened his menu. It continued the Christmas theme with items like the Merry Christmas Monte Cristo sandwich, Cherry Blitzens, Red-nosed Reuben, Holly Jolly Flapjacks, and the Silver Bell Burger with Pere Noel Fries.

Across the way, a man drinking hot chocolate was the spitting image of Santa Claus, if only he had a few more pounds on him. Was he a plant? A secret threat to the kids dining with their parents that the big guy was watching their behavior? Pretty good shtick if it was. Every town should have a restaurant like this.

Ryan nudged Zoe under the table with his foot, and then jerked his head in that direction, getting her to steal a glance.

Her face lit up.

"Must be the very best place to eat," he whispered.

Zoe nodded her head quickly. She craned her neck and then ducked behind her menu. "It looks like he is having the Silver Bell Burger."

"Well, then that's what I'm having," Ryan said, setting down his menu.

"Me, too!"

The perky woman came back over and set two glasses of water on the table. "What can I get you two today?"

"We're going to both have the Silver Bell Burger."

"Great choice." She scribbled on her pad. "Child-size for the young lady?"

"Yes please," Ryan said.

"Will you both be having the Pere Noel Fries with that?"

"Definitely," Zoe answered.

"Great. I'll get that order right in for you."

"Thank you." He handed her the menus.

Zoe lunged across the table, giggling. "Get it, Dad? 'Pere Noel' is the French Santa Claus. French Fries."

"You don't say."

"It's true. We learned it in school."

The food came fast considering how busy it was, and that was good, because they had a flight to catch. The woman had left the ticket when she'd served the food so they'd be able to eat and get back on the road.

Zoe ate with one eye on Santa.

"You ready?" he asked Zoe when they'd finished.

"Ready if you are." She bounced up and put her coat on, picking up the check from the table.

"You going to take care of that?" he teased.

"No! That's your department."

"Oh, I see." Ryan followed Zoe over to the counter. The pretty blonde wore a tiny gold locket around her neck and a nametag that read Carol. He remembered a similar necklace on the woman with the truck problems.

"Everything to your liking?" she asked warmly.

"Delicious," he said. "Does your daughter drive a red truck?"

"She does." She looked surprised. "You know Allie?"

"No. We briefly crossed paths, and she recommended this place for lunch. I'm glad she did. That was the best burger I'd had in a long time."

"I'm so glad you liked it." Carol handed him his change. "There you go."

"Thanks a lot."

Zoe seemed mesmerized by a snow globe that sat at the end of the counter.

"Merry Christmas," Carol said to her.

Zoe looked up. "Does this snow globe really grant wishes?"

Carol stepped over to her and leaned forward, laying a hand on the sign next to the snow globe. "Like the sign says, 'only if you know what your heart really wants.'"

Ryan watched the flash of confusion change to hope on his daughter's face.

"Where did it come from?"

Carol shrugged. "Nobody knows. One day, right after we opened this diner, it just showed up on our doorstep, along with that sign. It's been here ever since. People come from all over to make wishes. It's a tradition here in Evergreen."

"Have you ever made one?"

"A wish? I have." Carol's eyes filled with delight. "When I first got it, I wished to have a little girl just like you. And you know what? My wish came true."

Zoe beamed.

Carol had a way about her. Ryan hadn't seen that kind of smile on Zoe's face in a long time. Not since Sarah.

"Would you like to try it?" Carol urged her.

"Sure!"

"All right." Carol lifted the magical snow globe and held it out to Zoe. It was large and appeared heavy as Zoe took it with both hands.

"Careful, Zoe." How much did that kind of relic cost to replace? *Could* it be replaced? It appeared hand-carved. Zoe gave him the stink eye. Ryan noticed the Santa Claus-like man watching them.

After a moment's pause, she turned her back to him and the others like she was hiding something. She cradled the snow globe, then flipped it upside down and gave it a good shake. Then she righted it and watched the snowfall.

Zoe squeezed her eyes tight and made her wish.

Carol and Ryan shared a thoughtful glance. There was something special about the innocence of a child—the unchallenged belief in her heart and mind that he wished he still had.

Zoe spun back around with a broad smile and held the globe out to Ryan. "It's your turn, Dad."

"No, that's okay."

"Oh, c'mon, Dad. Don't be shy," Carol urged Ryan.

There were plenty of things he could ask for right now, like erasing the last year, but he wasn't about to put his faith in the magic of a snow globe. "I'm sure whatever Zoe wished for is good enough for both of us."

"Okay." Carol took the snow globe from Zoe and placed it back in its special spot.

"Thank you!"

Carol smiled gently. "You're welcome. Come back and tell us how that wish turned out, okay?"

"Okay! Bye!" Zoe said.

"Bye, honey."

"Merry Christmas," Ryan said. He held the door open for Zoe, the bells jingling as they stepped out onto the sidewalk together.

"Can't we stay a little longer?" Zoe pleaded.

"Zoe." Ryan clapped his hands on each of her shoulders. "The sooner we go to the airport, the sooner we get to Florida."

"Florida will be great. But…"

"But what?"

Zoe extended her arms. "Just look at this place."

"I promise. Florida is going to be so much fun, and you and me, we're going to have the best Christmas ever." But would any Christmas ever be as good as the ones they'd shared as a family? "Okay?"

Zoe gave him a brave smile. "Okay, Dad."

He opened the car door and prodded her along. "Okay! All right!" She climbed into the backseat. "In you go, kiddo." He closed the door.

He'd do anything for his daughter's happiness. He prayed he was doing the right thing. He kind of got why she'd wanted to hang around a little while here. This town did have a certain magic to it.

Ryan took in the festive Evergreen decorations. Sarah would've loved this; she would've had the same glimmer in her eyes that Zoe had right now. He glanced up at the sky. Clouds were rolling in, and the snow was already starting to get heavier. They needed to get on the road to beat the storm.

He pulled away from the curb, noticing the old red pickup truck coming back in his direction as he turned to head out of town.

Maybe he should've given in to Zoe's request to stay a little bit longer. He wouldn't have minded bumping into her one more time.

Allie parked her truck across the road from the Chris Kringle Kitchen. The snow had really started to fall, already leaving a soft layer on top of her suitcase in the bed of the truck.

Her parents walked out to meet her before she could even get out of the driver's seat. She gave the door handle a good tug and jumped out to meet them.

Dad was the first to say something. "Well," he said. "You're on your way?"

"Yes. All packed and ready to go." Excitement bubbled over. This was really it; only, with one glance toward her mom, her heart sank. "Mom…?" Allie knew better, and Mom's lower lip trembled.

"I'm not going to cry." Her mom lifted her chin, putting on a brave front. "You'll be back next week."

"Exactly," Allie said. "We'll have time for our big emotional goodbye then."

"Right." Carol tugged her jacket around her.

Allie waved her arms, beckoning Mom in for a hug. "Merry Christmas."

"Merry Christmas, sweetheart." She hugged her tightly. "You travel safely."

"I will." She turned to her father. "Bye, Daddy."

"Goodbye, sweetheart." He hugged her.

Mom rushed in and wrapped her arms around them both. "Family hug!" she said.

Emotion swept through Allie. "Okay, guys." She left before she changed her mind or started crying herself.

When she got to her truck, she turned around. Mom and Dad stood arm in arm, and Dad was choking back tears.

She heard Mom teasing him. "Chopping onions?"

"Yeah." He laughed.

Allie got back in her truck and waved a confident goodbye.

This was it. The beginning of her new life.

As Evergreen got smaller in her rearview mirror and she crossed the famous red covered bridge on her way out of town, reality sank in. She was spending Christmas away from everything she'd ever known the holiday to be. Her family. Her hometown. The Christmas festival, and her best friends.

In a few hours, she'd be in DC. With Spencer. She didn't have any other friends there yet. Just a new job waiting for her and an apartment that would be hers as soon as she signed the lease.

She drove along, thinking about her future as the windshield wipers swept the snow away in a steady rhythm.

What family traditions would she continue when

she moved? Would there be a tree farm nearby that she could go to and pick out a nice balsam or Fraser fir? Would they have someone on hand to cut it down, shake it, wrap it, and put it in her truck for her? Would the tree be so fresh that her fingers would stick together when she touched it? Now, that was the kind Christmas tree she liked.

Would there be cookie swaps with friends? Caroling to kick off the holiday season?

Or would this be the only Christmas she spent away?

There was no rule that said she couldn't still come home for Christmas no matter where she lived. There was comfort in that thought.

And her parents would come visit her in DC, too. There was so much to see. The museums. The theater. It would be fun to show them around the city. Maybe invite them down for the Cherry Blossom Festival. She'd only seen pictures, but it looked amazing—something not to miss. It would be interesting to see how festivals in Washington, D.C. compared to Evergreen, too.

By the time she got to the Burlington International Airport, the weather had settled in. The sky was an ominous gray, and the snow was beginning to pile quickly.

Yellow taxicabs lined up in front of the arrivals area, and people rushed here and there. Cars wove in and out like a well-choreographed dance, dropping off and picking up passengers.

Allie turned into the long-term parking area and searched for an open spot. She had to go to the very top floor to even find a place where she felt comfortable leaving her truck. Grandpa had given it to her in mint condition, and she didn't plan to change that. Even if it meant walking farther in the snow to protect it.

She got out and took a picture of the area sign to help her remember where she parked. Then she locked the door behind her and grabbed her bags, careful not to drag the wheels along the wooden stake side or the paint. The dry snow brushed right off, not even leaving a mark on her new luggage. The tan set with dark leather handles and trim had been a splurge. Kind of a look-the-part-of-a-well-traveled-city-girl treat to herself.

She slid the tote over the telescoping handle of the carry-on bag with wheels and then guided her luggage to the elevator. The bell rang and the doors slid open. A happy couple exited, holding hands and looking grateful to be reunited. She cruised in, standing against the back wall.

At the ground level, she hurried to the crosswalk, waving a thank you to the cars that had slowed to let her get by. She squinted against the heavy snow, flakes settling in the hair around her face. She blew her bangs from her cheek and rushed inside.

Terminal one was hectic. With the holidays upon them, even this small airport teemed with passengers anxious to reunite with family and begin their Christmas plans. She got in line to check in, noticing the electronic board behind the airline attendant showing several flights with delayed departures or late arrivals.

Thank goodness her flight was still on time. So far.

She headed straight to the security line with her carry-on bag. The long line snaked up and back down the corridor, corralling travelers like cows at the livestock market. She people-watched as she waited her turn and shuffled toward the screening area.

Finally through security, she walked down to the gates. It was one big, open area for several flights, and most of the seats were already occupied.

She found her gate and checked in with the agent. "Washington, D.C., please."

The gate agent handed her driver's license and ticket across the counter. A shiny gold aluminum Christmas tree shimmied on the counter as she moved her hand to take it. The whole terminal was decorated for Christmas with those same shiny miniature trees. Not too creative. "You're all set. Have a nice flight."

"Thank you." Allie was bursting at the seams, wanting to scream out to everyone that she was getting ready to move and start a whole new chapter in her life. Instead, she maintained composure and grabbed a seat near the gate, pulling her bags over next to her. She'd never done anything this brave or exciting before.

She overheard one of the gate agents telling travelers that several flights were delayed because of weather. That was probably why there were so many people milling around waiting. The flights were stacking up.

She tucked her bags close to her seat, leaving room for others to sit down for the longer-than-usual waits. As long as her flight didn't get canceled, she didn't mind a wait. It suited her just fine, in fact. This was the first time she'd had a moment to slow down in days. Enjoying the buzz of activity, the sound of someone mentioning Evergreen behind her caught her attention.

She turned to see if it was someone she knew.

Sitting right behind her was the father and daughter who'd miraculously helped her start her truck with the mere cross of fingers.

Chapter Nine

Ryan and Zoe made good time back to the airport. They dropped off the rental car and went straight to the terminal. They must have hit things just right, because when they got there, the lines to get through security moved quickly, putting them back on schedule.

They found a couple of empty spots together and got settled in the large multiple-gate seating area. His phone hadn't stopped pinging until he'd finally silenced it earlier, but now that they were sitting around waiting, with time to spare, he felt compelled to at least check his messages and make sure there wasn't anything urgent that needed his attention.

Zoe seemed happy enough people-watching at the gate. There was plenty to see, too. The gate agents rebooked passengers who'd missed connections, and emotions ran high when the new flight wasn't until the next day.

A silver-haired woman wearing a pretty white sweater and a knit scarf with a red, green, and white pattern was walking through the gate area, wishing passengers a Merry Christmas and giving out three-and-a-half-inch decorative poinsettias she'd hand knit herself. They could be worn as a pin or used as a tree ornament, she explained. She went on to tell everyone how delighted she was that her daughter and her new son-in-law were flying her down to Miami to visit her grandchildren. She hadn't seen them in almost a year.

Zoe seemed intrigued by the knitted flower, tucking it safely into her coat pocket.

Ryan listened to his messages. Most of them were just informative, but there was one he probably should return before they got on the plane. He dialed the number. Unfortunately, his colleague was in surgery. "Please tell him that Dr. Bellamy called. I'll be back after the New Year. Okay. Thanks so much." He glanced over at Zoe. "Last work call. I promise." This time, he meant it.

"It's okay, Dad. I'm having fun."

"You are?" He hoped so. So far it seemed pretty uneventful to him, but then, he'd been chasing down work calls all day. "What has been your favorite part so far?"

Zoe gave him an *are-you-kidding-me?* look. "Evergreen, of course!"

"Oh, hey!" a woman's voice came from nearby.

Ryan and Zoe turned to see the woman with the truck that wouldn't start back in Evergreen sitting right behind them.

"Well, if it isn't my mechanic and her assistant."

She twisted around in her seat, resting her elbow on the back of her chair with a friendly smile.

"Hey! What are you doing here?" Ryan was shocked to see her again. Maybe that magic snow globe had granted one of his wishes without him even shaking it.

"Taking an airplane." She wrinkled her nose.

Well, if that wasn't a dumb thing of him to ask. Of course she was here to get on a plane. "We are, too," Ryan said, and Zoe giggled. "We're going to Florida."

"Washington D.C. I'm Allie, by the way."

Allie. That was a nice name. It suited her. "I'm Ryan, and this is Zoe."

"Hi, Zoe," Allie said. "How was lunch?"

"It was great! And I made a wish on the snow globe." Zoe raised a brow. "I'm pretty sure it's what my heart wanted."

Allie's face lit up. "You know, my grandpa used to say, 'the heart knows what it wants even when the head doesn't.' So, what did you wish for?"

Zoe shook her head in an emphatic no. "I can't tell you or else it won't come true." But then her face contorted in disappointment. "But I'm starting to worry that it's not going to come true anyway."

"Hmm. Well, maybe you should wish for it again— give it a little turbo boost," Allie recommended with exuberance.

"But I don't have the snow globe."

"Oh, it's pretty powerful," Allie said with certainty. "I bet it'll be able to hear you from all the way over here."

Ryan was impressed by the way she interacted with

Zoe, and Zoe seemed to buy into the idea of a turbo boost.

Zoe considered that for a second, then with a nod, she spun around in her chair. She raised both hands and crossed her fingers. With determination on her face, she squeezed her eyes tight.

He looked to Allie, smiling appreciatively.

Allie gave him a she-is-the-cutest-kid-ever look, but before he uttered a word, a voice came blasting through the speaker system overhead.

"Ladies and gentleman in the terminal, I'm sorry to report that due to heavy snow, we are closing the runway and cancelling all flights."

Disappointment dominoed through the building as travelers realized what that meant to them and their holiday plans. Allie's jaw dropped.

Ryan glanced over at the blue electronic flight tracker board above the gate desk. Flights began flipping from ON TIME to CANCELLED, and before he knew it, there was a blackout bingo of cancelled flights.

"Oh, come on." All Ryan wanted was to give his little girl a happy Christmas. One she could remember that might dim the sadness they'd gone through last year. Why was the universe working against him?

There were moans and groans from everyone, but if he didn't know better, he'd have thought he saw a smile on Zoe's face before she turned around. She was such a good sport.

People scattered in half panic, trying to figure out

the best way to salvage their trips. Some were on the phone rebooking; others were lined twenty-five deep at the gate counter, demanding to be put on a plane or get their money back. A couple of guys standing nearby talked about renting an SUV and driving out of the mess.

Ryan told himself to relax. True, he was anxious to get to Florida and get this Christmas started, but they still had a few days before the cruise ship set sail. If they got out tomorrow, or even the next day, they'd miss the land portion of the trip, but everything else would still work out. Getting upset would only make things worse for Zoe, so he put his best foot forward.

He texted his office manager and asked her to get them rebooked on a flight tomorrow. Any time of day would do. Then he turned to Zoe. "Come on, kiddo." He grabbed the luggage and gestured for her to fall in step with him.

"Are we going home?"

"No way. That wouldn't be any fun." He wheeled their luggage out of the gate area and through the glass doors to the Burlington Central Hotel. It was convenient that they didn't even have to leave the airport building to get there. Unfortunately, a lot of other travelers had the same idea, but this line was a lot shorter than the rebooking line.

Luckily, when it was his turn at the registration desk, they had rooms in the process of being cleaned, and he was lucky enough to get the last double room.

"We'll stay up late and watch movies. It'll be great," he said to Zoe.

"Okay. Do you think we could get something to eat first?"

"Sure."

The desk clerk pointed to the fancy dining room behind them. "We're serving French cuisine in our restaurant there, or"—she leaned forward and lowered her voice—"the bistro next door at the airport just before the security gate has the most awesome grilled ham-and-cheese sandwich. It's my personal favorite."

"Grilled cheeses," Zoe and Ryan said in unison. "Thanks so much," Ryan added.

Zoe spun her bright purple suitcase around and led the way back into the terminal to the diner.

Chapter Ten

A llie walked back into the airport and as soon as she did, she spotted Ryan and Zoe standing near the hostess station of the airport coffee shop waiting for a table. "Did you get a hotel?"

"We did. Yes," Ryan said. "We're just going to grab a bite to eat. Did you?"

"I'm going to head back to Evergreen. It's not that far."

"Are you sure you're okay to drive in this storm?"

Allie rolled her eyes. "Oh, please. My truck has seen way worse than this. Hopefully, tomorrow, everything will be back up and running again."

Zoe nudged her dad. "Does the plane getting cancelled mean we aren't going to Florida?"

"No," Ryan reassured her. "We'll still have plenty of time to catch our cruise."

Zoe didn't seem thrilled.

"Oh, wow. A cruise?" Allie mused for Zoe's benefit. "That sounds like a fancy Christmas. Certainly a lot warmer."

"Yeah. It'll be great," Zoe said.

Allie realized she didn't want to exchange goodbyes with these two yet, but there wasn't anything else to say. "Well, it was nice to meet you."

"Nice meeting you, too." Ryan looked into her eyes as if he were going to say something. Finally, he said, "Maybe we'll see you around here tomorrow."

I hope so. "Yeah. And if not, Merry Christmas."

"Merry Christmas, Allie!" Zoe waved with one hand, clutching her purple roller bag with the other.

Allie waved goodbye and headed for the exit as the hostess came to seat Ryan and Zoe.

"Yes. Two, please," she heard him say.

She glanced over her shoulder one last time before exiting the terminal. It would be nice if their paths crossed again tomorrow.

She hadn't been away from her truck long enough to need to reference the picture she'd taken with her phone just a couple of hours ago to help her find it. But, having parked on the rooftop, when she did get there, her truck already had a good bit of fresh snow covering the windshield. She put her luggage inside the cab this time and dialed Spencer on his direct line.

"Allie?"

"Hi. Bad news. The flight got cancelled because of the snow."

He made an audible sigh. "I was just heading out to the airport to pick you up."

"I'm sorry. It'll be sometime tomorrow. Hopefully."

"I'm working tomorrow."

What does that have to do with anything? "That's okay. I can get a cab from the airport."

There was an odd silence. "No second thoughts, right?"

The question surprised her. "Spencer. I didn't cause the snow. Let me just get there. Everything is going to be fine."

"Sure. Of course. Call me tomorrow?"

"Of course."

She disconnected the call and considered it for a moment. *Was* she having second thoughts? Or was the universe trying to tell her something with the flight being cancelled? She shook her head. *It's winter. This is what happens in this kind of weather.*

Ready to get back home and do this all over again tomorrow, she tucked her phone away and started her truck. Well, she tried to, but it wouldn't do more than that tired, droning groan again. "Oh, no, come on. Really? I thought you wanted me to be in Evergreen!" She smacked the steering wheel.

Calming herself down, she gave the truck a little time to rest before she tried again.

After another thirty minutes of unsuccessful attempts, she was getting cold, and it was becoming clear this old truck wasn't ready to leave. She'd probably flooded the engine trying for so long by now anyway, so she gave up and decided it was time to go back inside to warm up.

It was like déjà vu as she took the elevator down

from the parking garage. She jogged across the crosswalk and went back into the airport.

The warmth of the lobby was welcoming. She brushed away the snow from her coat. A nice cup of hot chocolate and something to eat would be good right about now. Perhaps it would also let her blow off that feeling that had been nagging her ever since she'd spoken with Spencer. That call had bothered her, although she couldn't quite put her finger on why.

She walked over to the diner. "Can I sit anywhere?" she asked the hostess, who was walking up just as she got there.

"Sure." The hostess pointed to her right toward several open tables.

"Thanks." Allie hadn't even gotten past the second booth when she heard her name.

"Allie!"

Her heart leaped at the sound of Zoe's voice. They'd just finished their meal. "Hey there."

"I thought you were going back to Evergreen." Ryan stated the obvious.

"I was. I've been trying to get my truck started for the last hour."

"Do you want us to pretend to fix it again?" He raised his hand and crossed his fingers, sending Zoe into a fit of giggles.

"Thank you, but no." Allie loved their sense of humor. "I'm going to grab a bite to eat and then I'll try again. If it still doesn't start, I'll get a hotel for the night."

"Come sit with us, Allie!" Zoe scooched over in the booth. "You can tell us about Evergreen."

She looked to Ryan to make sure he was okay with her joining them, and he was nodding, too, so she slid into the booth next to Zoe. "What would you like to know?"

"Well?" Zoe thought for a moment. "What do you do for Christmas?"

"Oh." Allie settled into the seat. "Every year, we have this big festival." The waitress brought her a menu. "Thank you," she said, then continued her story. "With food, games, and a choir. People come from all over the place. It's the town's biggest tradition."

"What do you do in Evergreen?" Ryan asked.

"I run a veterinarian practice." She loved talking about her work. "Or, I did." It was hard to get used to saying that. "But now I'm moving to Washington D.C. for a new job and…for a change of scenery." *Why did I put it that way? Am I having second thoughts about Spencer?*

Zoe's smile drooped. "So you're not going to spend Christmas in Evergreen?"

"No." Nostalgia flooded Allie's heart. "For the first time in…forever." She hadn't realized just how much she was going to miss the festival—and Evergreen—until now.

"The festival sounds like fun," Zoe said.

"It is." Allie couldn't contain her enthusiasm for all the memories that flooded back, but then she caught him staring at her, kind of nodding toward his daughter. "But…not as fun as Florida," she said, trying to make it sound awesome. "I mean, come on. The beach?" She gave Zoe her best convincing look, but she was with the girl on this one. Who wanted to go to a sunshiny spot for the holidays? Maybe if Allie had grown up someplace warm, she would've felt differently, but in her mind, Christmas and snow went together like cookies and milk.

"Yeah. It'll be great." Zoe flashed her dad a smile, then popped an arm on the table, ready to chat more with Allie.

Allie was convinced Zoe's smile was forced. "Hey, can I show you something?"

"Sure," Zoe said.

"Check it out." Allie took her paper napkin from under her silverware and pulled it in front of her. "You do a fold. And then another fold." She made one more triangle, then smoothed out the seams. "And then you make these tiny little tears. Little triangles." She ripped the pieces around the edges of the folded napkin, letting the excess fall to the table. "And then…" She unfolded the napkin and held it up. "You unfold to reveal the magical snowflake!"

"Cool!"

Allie turned the paper snowflake over in her hands. "Yeah, my mom taught me that. She said this way I could always carry the magic of the Evergreen Christmas with me wherever I go."

"Neat!" Zoe was delighted. "My mom used to make a lot of our Christmas decorations."

Allie heard the land mine in that comment.

There was a brief silence, and Allie realized that her troubles with Spencer were insignificant compared to this. She couldn't imagine being without her mom. She wanted to ask what happened but knew the topic was a sensitive one by the look in Zoe and Ryan's eyes.

She leaned in closer to Zoe. "Do you want to learn how to do it yourself?"

"Sure!"

"Yeah. I'll show you." She gestured to Ryan. "Napkin."

"Napkin," he said like a doctor in surgery.

"All right. Your turn." Allie handed the napkin to Zoe. "Fold it in half."

"Like this?"

When Allie looked up, she caught Ryan's eye—he was smiling at them. He mouthed, *Thank you*.

He was so lucky to have a sweet daughter like Zoe. It must be hard to be a single parent, but he seemed to be doing a great job. She nodded and turned her full attention back to Zoe while he watched them with his chin propped up on his hands.

The waitress came over. "Are you ready to order?"

"I think I'll have a cup of cocoa, and can I get a sandwich? Theirs looked good."

"Got it. It'll be right out."

"Thank you." Allie watched Zoe's progress. "Oh, you're a natural."

"I learn fast."

"The key is tearing those little triangle pieces. Any

shapes, really. I mean, no two snowflakes are supposed to be alike."

Zoe ripped several more shapes around the edges. "Like this?"

"Looks good. Ready to do the reveal?" Allie prompted.

Zoe unfolded the napkin with care, then held up her finished snowflake.

"It's beautiful," her dad said.

"Better than mine. I love it."

"You can keep this one." Zoe handed her the snowflake. "Since you won't be here for Christmas."

"You are the most thoughtful girl." She looked into those big brown eyes. "I'm so glad we bumped into each other today."

"Me too," he said.

The waitress came out with Allie's order and refilled Zoe and Ryan's drinks. "Can I get you anything else?"

"That'll be all. Just the check," Allie said. They chatted more about Evergreen, how they decorated like this at Christmas every year and details about the fun events. She told them about the toy store in town, too. "There are lots of great shops on Main Street. Evergreen is small, but we pack a lot of good stuff into our town, and the people are awesome."

"Sounds like it."

Allie moved her plate to the edge of the table, and the waitress dropped her bill off. "Thank you."

"We'll have to stop in Evergreen every time we go back to Grandma and Grandpa's. It was kind of right on the way."

"That's true," Ryan said. "They live just over the line in New York. Less than two hours, and the ferry breaks up the ride. I'm surprised I'd never stopped in Evergreen before. It's kind of a hidden gem tucked away with just the one sign."

"It is." That it wasn't all that well-known was part of the beauty of it. She was glad to be going home to sleep in her own bed in Evergreen tonight. Talking about her hometown had made her miss it already, and she hadn't even left yet. "I'm just…" Allie got up and went to pick up her bill, but Ryan grabbed it. "Thank you. I'm going to go see if I can get my truck started. If I can't, I'll get a room for the night."

"It's probably time for us to go to our room, too, Zoe. Are you ready?"

"Yes, sir."

Ryan took out his wallet and dropped a couple of twenties on the table. "That should cover it all."

"Thank you." Allie got up and followed behind them until they veered off at the hotel.

"Drive safely," Ryan said.

She raised her hand in a wave as she stepped outside. The air was brisk, but it seemed clean and fresh after being inside the crowded restaurant.

The parking garage was clearing out a little. Folks must've been heading back home since the flights were cancelled, or had decided to drive to stay on schedule. At least the roads weren't bad. Vermont did a great job keeping the main highways clear.

Back on the roof of the parking deck, she gave her

truck a silent pep talk the whole walk over to it. She patted the hood in encouragement, then slid behind the wheel. "C'mon. Let's get started," she said as she twisted the key in the ignition.

But no luck. She tried and tried, but the truck refused to start. It was too cold to sit and mess with it now that it was starting to get dark. She'd have to stay at the hotel.

She let out a sigh, then gathered her things. She'd waited so long now that she hoped she'd be able to even get a room. The lobby was busy, but she was able to get to the desk quickly. Hopefully a good sign.

"Please tell me you have a room for tonight."

The desk clerk smiled. "I have one left. Someone just cancelled their reservation."

"Thank goodness." Allie pulled out her wallet and handed the clerk her driver's license. "My truck wouldn't start. I'm stranded."

"I'm so sorry." The clerk went to town typing on her computer, then pulled a piece of paper from the printer and handed her the register. "You're in luck. King-size bed. Initial here and here for me, and I'll need a credit card."

Allie handed over her credit card, not even bothering to ask what the nightly rate was, because at this point, what did it matter?

"I've got you in this room." The clerk pointed to the number on the front of the small white folder. "Elevators are right over there. Wi-Fi is free. The password is inside the card pocket."

"Thank you," Allie said.

"Breakfast starts at six and runs until nine in the morning."

"Bonus. Thanks again. You saved my day." She walked over to the elevator and took it up to the fifth floor.

The room was very nice. The king-size bed looked so inviting with its deep piles of white linens. There was an excellent view of the airport, which was a little eerie with everything at a standstill. Allie turned on the bedside lamp and dialed her parents' restaurant. "Hi, Dad. Bad news. My flight got cancelled."

"Oh, no."

"Then the truck wouldn't start."

"Do you want me to come get you?"

"No. I got a room here at the hotel airport tonight. Hopefully, I'll be able to fly out tomorrow morning."

She heard him relaying the message to others. Nothing new. Seemed the whole town always knew her business.

Dad came back on the line. "Ezra said you know it's bad if they've closed the airport."

Michelle's voice rose in the background. "Luckily, we're not landing planes, we're just having a festival."

"My first festival," Ezra reminded everyone, "and we get a blizzard. If we'd had an app, we'd have known that."

"Oh, no," Allie said. Would Ezra ever give up on that app idea? Now probably wasn't the time to mention her Bovine Translator App.

"Ezra, relax," Dad said. "Everything will be just fine."

"Sounds like you and Mom have your hands full," Allie said.

"Business as usual," he said. "Keep us posted, and let us know if you need our help."

"I will, Daddy." She hung up the phone. She set her suitcase on the dresser and took out a pair of pajamas. She slipped into them and then got right into bed and turned the television to the Hallmark Channel. So what if she was getting a later start on her new adventure than she planned? She couldn't turn her nose up at a relaxing night like this. She switched the light off and laid back against the pillows. With all the hope and warmth those movies brought to her heart, she watched two back-to-back, then turned off the television, pulled the covers tightly around her, and drifted off into a peaceful slumber.

Allie woke up early, as if it was any other work day, even though she had no place to be. She'd never been one who needed an alarm clock. She got up, padded over to the window, and pulled back the drapes.

Her mood plummeted. Nothing was moving out on the runways yet. Not great news.

She checked her phone for any updates. Unfortunately, today's flights had already been cancelled, too. She logged into the airline app. They had rescheduled her on a flight the following day. Spencer was going to be disappointed too.

She ought to take advantage of the hotel and sleep

in until checkout time. She rolled over, telling herself to relax, but it wasn't her nature to lay around. She tossed. Turned. Tried to count sheep; in her head, she began examining and vaccinating them, which wasn't helpful when trying to fall back asleep.

Finally, she gave in and got out of bed. She repacked her pajamas and changed clothes, then headed down to the lobby to get breakfast and extend her stay another night.

Chapter Eleven

Ryan had already struck out getting his stay here at the Burlington Central Hotel extended. It seemed other travelers had been less optimistic than he was when things had gone haywire yesterday, booking two nights to begin with. That was something to keep in mind if he was ever in this situation again.

Having just called every hotel in the area and not coming up with anything, not even an expensive option, it was becoming clear that he and Zoe might be sleeping in the airport tonight. That wasn't appealing at all.

He phoned his office and had them start looking for an Airbnb nearby, or the possibility of flying out of a different airport tomorrow. Albany was about a three-hour drive south, but if they could get a room at that hotel, it might be an alternative.

All he wanted was to give Zoe the best Christmas ever, but Mother Nature was definitely making it more difficult than he'd ever imagined. He wouldn't give up

that easily, though. He'd come up with a solution…
somehow.

Ryan heard Allie's cheerful voice across the way.
He turned and saw her standing at the front desk with
her back to him. She was talking to the clerk who was
emphatically moving her head from left to right. He
felt Allie's pain. He'd just gone through that, too. No
room at the inn.

"Thank you so much for checking," Allie said. "No
problem."

But there was a problem, and he was having the
same one.

Allie spotted them and walked over. "With all the
flights that were cancelled, there are no more rooms.
They won't let me stay another night."

"The same with us." Ryan held his phone in the
air, and then shoved it back into his pocket. "And
there are no rooms anywhere, it seems."

"I'm going to see if I can get my truck started,"
she said. "If I can, you're welcome to come back to
Evergreen."

Zoe bounced up on her toes like she was getting
ready to do a swan dive. "Yes!" She quickly looked at
her dad and toned it down. "I mean…yeah, we *could*
go to Evergreen again, right, Dad?"

"That's very nice, but where would we even stay?
Is there a hotel or…"

Allie cocked her head. "Sort of."

Sort of? It was a yes-or-no question. Then again, in
his current situation, "sort of" was an improvement.

And he didn't really care where they stayed as long as they were safe and comfortable. Those airport lobby chairs were barely tolerable for sitting, much less sleeping.

She wiggled her brows in a playful way, then pulled out her phone and scrolled through her contacts.

Ryan heard the woman on the other end of Allie's call answer with a cheerful-sounding "Merry Christmas."

"Barbara? It's Allie."

"Hi, Allie."

"Am I calling at a bad time? You sound out of breath."

"No. I was hanging the wreath on the door and putting more decorations out front. What's up?"

"I'm calling because all the flights going out of Burlington have been cancelled and there's literally no room at the inn. I've made friends with these nice folks who were heading to Florida for Christmas, only now they're stranded."

"Oh no. That's terrible," Barbara said. "I'm so sorry."

"I know you aren't planning to open for a couple more weeks, but would that mean you have a vacancy for a nice man and his daughter for the night?"

Barbara's excitement came through the line. "Yes! It would be wonderful to have them stay here. Just as long as they know it's not quite finished yet. But I can easily make up a guest room."

"Oh, Barbara, that would be great." Allie gave Ryan the thumbs up.

"Wonderful. Okay, I'll see you then. My first guests! I'm so excited. Bye!"

Allie hung up her phone. "You are the first guests to ever stay at Barbara's Country Inn. She needs you to know it's not all the way finished. She doesn't officially open for a couple of weeks."

"We're not picky," he said. "We'll even help." Zoe nodded with exuberance.

"I'm sure you won't even be able to tell it's not ready for business. I hear she's doing amazing things with that place. She's such a neat lady. You'll enjoy meeting her, and it's walking distance from my house. I can give you a ride back to the airport tomorrow."

"I'm sure the inn will be fine." He was thankful to have a place to stay, and being in Evergreen again would be fun for Zoe. That town had made a good first impression on his little girl. She was clearly eager to get back to it for another peek.

"Now, we just have to get the truck to start."

"Good thing you have your mechanics with you," Zoe teased.

"You're right. Come on." Allie led the way to the parking deck. "Okay, guys, you can throw your luggage in the back."

Ryan picked up their two suitcases and put them in the back of the truck. "Hop on in, kiddo." He opened the door for Zoe, and she scrambled into the middle of the bench seat.

Allie put her bags in the back and got in, too.

With all three of them piled into the front seat,

they shared a hopeful glance and then Allie turned the key.

He hadn't even realized he was holding his breath, but when the truck started on the first try, Ryan let out one big exhale. They all cheered, and finally, things seemed to be going his way. What a nice change of events.

"All right, guys. Buckle up," Allie said. "Evergreen, here we come!"

Chapter Twelve

Allie knew the route from Burlington to Evergreen well, and her old truck took command of the highway like it was a sunny day.

Zoe craned her neck to get a better view of a horse-drawn sleigh being pulled through the snow on a side road. "This is so neat." It was fun to see things through the fresh eyes of a child. She might have taken that for granted if Zoe hadn't been here.

"Allie, my dad's a people doctor, and you're a pet doctor. So, you're kind of the same."

Ryan reasoned, "Well, except my patients can tell me where it hurts."

"Oh, well you've obviously never met an unhappy reindeer." She flapped her hand in the international talking symbol. "You get a lot of this." Allie's phone interrupted their fun. She glanced at the display. "Ooh, it's Henry." She pressed the button for speakerphone. "Can you hold this?" she asked Zoe.

"Yes." Zoe held the phone up so Allie could talk without taking her hands off the wheel.

"Hey, Henry."

"Doc! Buttercup is in labor."

"No. I told you she's not due for another week."

"But she's mooing like crazy…"

"Really?" *Didn't we just go through this?*

"Oh yeah, and loud." Worry hung in each word.

"All right. Well, I'm actually headed back into town right now."

"You're coming back?"

"No. Not exactly. It's a long story. I'll be there as soon as I can."

"Thanks, Doc."

"Bye," she said, and then whispered to Zoe, "You can hang it up." Allie straightened at the wheel. "Well, guys, I'm afraid we're going to have to take a little detour."

Ryan looked at her like he was wondering what in the world he'd gotten them into, but she had a feeling Zoe would enjoy the side trip.

A few miles up the road, Allie turned off to the right and headed for the countryside. She pointed across the way. "About a mile down that road is the Christmas tree farm my grandpa always took me to. Best one in Vermont."

Zoe pressed her face against the glass, amazed by the perfect grid of Christmas trees in all sizes. "Dad, we should get ours there."

"It's a long way to go for a tree," he pointed out.

"Every year, my grandpa would let me pick out our tree. I've always had a soft spot for the runt of the litter, so I'd pick the smallest, neediest-looking thing on the farm."

Ryan smiled gently. "That's actually kind of noble."

"My mother never thought so. She'd just sigh at the tangle of branches we'd drag in. I'm confident in saying that if it had been Dad's dad instead of hers taking me shopping for that tree, she would never have allowed those little scrawny trees in the door."

"So you were looking out for the underdog. And still are," he said.

"Dog? Veterinarian?" Allie shook her head, pointing a wise-guy finger in his direction. "I see what you did there. Nicely done." He laughed at his own corny joke.

Zoe clapped her hands wildly. "Wow, Dad! Look at all the cows. And horses."

"This is beautiful country," he said.

"Here we are," Allie announced. She took the familiar path back to the old barn.

"This is quite an operation," Ryan remarked.

"Henry's family has owned this property for generations." She followed the road to the barn, and then parked. "Come along. You'll love Henry. And you're not going to want to miss this."

Zoe tumbled out of the truck behind Allie, who slipped on her work coat. "This way to the stalls."

"Hey, Henry."

"Thanks so much for coming, Doc."

"You're welcome. Meet Zoe and Ryan while I look at what we've got here." The three of them made quick friends as she checked Buttercup. Her udder was full, and had been for days, but now her teats had lost that Coke-bottle shape and were extended. She placed her hand on Buttercup's left side, feeling for movement.

Buttercup mooed, and Allie felt the contraction, then put on her gloves and did a quick check. Sure enough, she was fully dilated, and the good news was the calf's nose and hooves were right there where they were supposed to be. "Yeah. Henry, you were right. She's in labor."

Henry stood with his arms folded. "Told you I knew their moos."

Ryan sprang into action. "What can I do to help?"

"Henry, you go get me a big bucket of hot water. And Ryan, bring me my bag."

"You got it," he said, heading for the truck.

"What can I do to help?" Zoe asked.

"You can take apart a bale of hay, because we're going to make a little nest for the baby."

Buttercup mooed, seeming to agree with the plan.

"You got it." Zoe ran over to a stack of hay bales in the alleyway. One was already open, and she carried a whopping armful back into the stall and then went back for more. Then she proceeded to arrange it for their new arrival. "How big will the baby cow be?"

"As big as you."

Zoe pulled her lips into a tight line. "Wow. Then I'd better make this bed a little bigger." She went back to work, fluffing the hay.

Ryan came back with Allie's bag. He looked so

proud of his daughter, who was taking her job very seriously.

It warmed Allie's heart to be able to share a moment like this with them. She sidled up closer to Ryan. "You know, Buttercup will do all the work if all goes according to plan. I just wanted Zoe to feel like a part of it." She remembered the first time she'd ever seen a calf born. She'd been helping her Grandpa that day, riding along on his farm visits, when they'd gotten called for an emergency. That visit had been chaotic and they'd almost lost the cow, but it had a happy ending and had been such a special day to her. She still remembered it like it was yesterday, right down to what she'd been wearing. Her grandpa had earned superhero of her heart that day.

"I know. Thank you, Allie."

"It'll be a wait-and-see for a while," she said. "You sure you don't mind hanging around? I could get someone to take you over to Barbara's if you'd rather."

"Are you kidding?" he laughed. "Zoe would never forgive me if I let her miss this."

They stepped out of the stall to give Buttercup some privacy as she mooed her way through the contractions.

"Allie! Allie!" Zoe climbed over the stall and slid to a stop next to her. "She had the baby!"

Ryan, Zoe, and Henry watched in proud amazement at the wobbling black-and-white calf making gentle sounds with its mother. Allie checked out the newborn calf with Henry standing close by. She examined the calf, made sure her airways were clear, and then dipped her navel in iodine to ward off infection.

Allie then turned and checked Buttercup's udder. "Everything looks good."

Zoe kneeled down next to the calf. "She's so beautiful."

"She is. She's awesome." Allie agreed. "Thanks for your help."

"Me?" She laid her hand on the calf's still-damp back.

"Yeah, you. I couldn't have done this without you," Allie said.

Henry squatted next to Zoe. "Allie has a point, Zoe. I think you should be the one to name her."

Zoe's mouth dropped and her eyes widened. "Okay, but this is big." She was so serious. "I'm going to need a minute."

Henry chuckled.

"What should I call you?" Zoe stroked the calf.

Buttercup mooed, but softly this time. The tiny calf responded with her own noises.

Ryan smiled at Allie, which made her smile even bigger. This was such a neat thing to be able to share with them, and Ryan and Zoe being here made it even more meaningful for her, too.

Ryan spoke quietly. "Thank you."

"For what?"

"For…making Zoe feel so special."

"There's lots of special in that moment. It's nice to spread it around." Overcome by the experience herself, she blinked back a tear. "I'm really going to miss this," she said with a heavy heart.

"After seeing how good you are with animals, I have a feeling that they're going to miss you, too." His words were tender, and then he turned back to watch his daughter with the calf.

What a nice thing to say. Ryan was something special. Kind. Gentle. Thoughtful.

"Hey, everybody. I've decided," Zoe announced.

Allie and Ryan stepped closer to Henry and Zoe in the stall.

Zoe said, "The baby's name should be...Snowflake."

Henry let out a hearty laugh. "Perfect."

"I love it," Allie said, and Buttercup mooed in what sounded like an approval.

"Come on. Dinner time, Snowflake." Henry helped the calf get steady on her feet and amble toward Buttercup.

"Thanks, Doc." Henry shook her hand. "And to you, Ryan and Zoe."

Allie changed out of her work coat. Once the baby had nursed, everything else would happen on its own. "I think we can leave now," she said.

"Zoe, we need to go," Ryan said.

But Zoe didn't even make an attempt to move. She was still stroking the calf while she tried to nurse for the first time. "But I love Snowflake!"

"I swear," he said. "She's going to try to smuggle that thing in her suitcase."

Zoe reluctantly stood, then gave the newborn

calf an unsteady hug before coming out of the stall and locking the door behind her. "That was amazing, Dad." She ran up to his side.

"It sure was." He put his arm around her shoulder.

"And look at the snow now! It's even harder." Zoe held out her gloved hands, catching snowflakes.

"Henry, if your herd gets any bigger, you might have to keep this old barn."

"Or finally put that new barn to good use," Henry said.

Allie's phone rang. "Hold on one second." She stepped away to take the call. "Allie Shaw. Whoa! Ezra. Calm down. I can't understand you."

Ezra filled her in on the recent disaster. A pipe had broken in the town hall building, flooding the entire place. It was unfortunate they didn't have the funds for an emergency fix, since the Annual Christmas Festival was, in fact, the fundraiser for the town hall preservation fund. "It's a mess. It's like a skating rink in there," Ezra said. "We're going to have to cancel the festival."

She turned back to Ryan and Henry. "Oh, guys. We may not be able to have the festival."

Ezra sounded beaten down. "Well, the only way we're going to have it this year is if we find someplace else to do it."

"Somewhere else to do it? Where?" Allie couldn't imagine how Michelle and Ezra felt right now. The whole town looked forward to the event.

In the background, she heard Michelle saying, "There's no place in town with enough space."

Allie couldn't believe their bad luck. Wishing for an idea, she looked up...

And the answer was right in front of her. That new barn of Henry's was in shipshape. Not a single animal had even entered the brand-new building. They'd have nothing to do except decorate.

She turned to Henry. "Henry...I think I've got an idea about how we can put your new barn to really good use. How would you like to host the Christmas Festival?"

"Sure thing," Henry said without hesitation.

Chapter Thirteen

Allie gave Ezra the good news. Henry had agreed to let Evergreen use his new barn for the Christmas Festival this year. Free of charge. There was plenty of room, and plenty of parking, too.

There was even more room at the barn than there was at town hall. They'd salvage the decorations they could get out safely, and then have everyone work together to turn Henry's barn into a winter wonderland.

Ezra and Michelle both seemed happy with the idea. Allie hung up her phone and turned to Henry. "Thanks so much, Henry. You're an angel."

Henry's cheeks flushed. "You know how much I love the festival. I'm happy to help." His face got serious. "This doesn't mean I'll be ineligible to win the Snowball Bash, will it? I've got a title to defend."

"Not at all! You have at it," Allie teased.

It had been a long day, but a fulfilling one, and it would be getting dark soon.

Allie, Ryan, and Zoe piled back into her truck, and Allie drove them over to Barbara's Country Inn. She parked on the street in front of the charming house, then helped Zoe get her bag while Ryan got the rest of their things.

As they walked up to the house, even Allie was impressed with how festive everything looked. Every gabled window, rafter, and peak on the house was lit with white lights. The front porch was decorated so beautifully. The wreath was huge and fluffy. Barbara must've made it herself. Every tree, and practically every shrub, sparkled too. Santa himself would want to pit stop here after a long night's work.

What did Barbara consider "finished"? Allie may have finally met her match. Someone who loved Christmas as much as she did.

As they wheeled the luggage up the lighted sidewalk, Zoe stopped in her tracks. "Wow, Dad. Look at this. It's beautiful!"

A wooden sign painted in forest green hung from two chains on a tall wrought iron bracket with *Barbara's Country Inn* in fancy white scripted letters.

Allie was pleased Ryan and Zoe were so happy with it. "Go on. Let's go inside."

Zoe led the way. "Yeah! Let's go inside."

Barbara greeted them at the door. The smell of fresh cookies filled the front hall. "Come in! Welcome." Barbara swept her arm wide for them to enter.

Allie hadn't been inside since the housewarming party a couple of months ago, and that was before all of the renovations had been done. She was absolutely gobsmacked by how magnificent it looked. The inside of the inn was ready for both guests and Christmas with beautiful decorations everywhere.

Barbara led them through the lobby. "Since we're not officially open, there's no check-in process for you. I'm so pleased to have you here. My very first guests. Let me show you around." She walked through a set of double doors that led to a room in a ruby jewel tone. "This is the dining room."

Ryan put down the luggage.

"It's like we're in a storybook," Zoe exclaimed.

"When did you have time to decorate?" Allie said in awe.

"Oh, I've been working nonstop. The only thing I haven't been able to do is get a tree."

"I haven't gotten one, either," Allie said, forgetting for a split second that she'd planned to be away for the holiday.

"Well, the inn looks beautiful, Barbara." Ryan hugged Zoe close at his side. "Thank you so much for letting us stay here."

"Are you kidding? I'm so happy to have you. Do you want to see the rest of the place?"

"Yes," both Ryan and Allie said.

"Okay." Barbara walked toward the hall with Zoe at her heels.

"You know what, why don't you two go on ahead," Ryan said. "We'll catch up in a moment."

"Okay," Zoe said. "Bye."

Barbara and Zoe went into the adjacent living room while Allie stayed back with Ryan.

"Listen. I just wanted to say thank you one more time for taking such good care of us today."

"It's my pleasure. Hopefully, the airport will be open tomorrow so you guys can be back on your way."

"Yeah, although as far as detours go, this has been a pretty eventful one. I doubt we'll see too many cows on the cruise."

"Oh. A cow cruise. That sounds fun," she teased. "So, if you don't mind me asking…why Florida?"

"No, I…" Ryan hesitated a beat, but then he took a deep breath and dove in. "Sarah…my wife…she died last year just before Christmas. Which was really hard, you know? Every candy cane, every Christmas tree, was like a reminder. So, anyway, this year, I wanted Zoe to have sunshine and palm trees in Florida. Stay as far away from Christmas as possible."

Allie pulled her lips to one side in kind of a grimace. "And then I brought you to the Vermont version of the North Pole."

"North Pole adjacent. It's like a suburb of the North Pole."

"Yeah, like right there on the commuter line." She rolled her eyes.

"Right there," he agreed with a laugh.

"Listen, if it's any consolation, I think she's okay. More than okay. She's an awesome kid."

"Thanks," Ryan said. "I wish I could take credit for it, but that was all Sarah. Even after I pulled back from patient care, I worked so much that…"

She wanted to comfort and reassure him somehow.

"I think you're too hard on yourself. You don't have to be Super Dad to be a good dad."

"Well…anyway, thank you."

"Yeah." She'd never met anyone quite like him. She was thankful for the weather-related events that had forced their paths to cross, if even just for the great memories they'd made today. It brought her so much joy to be able to share Evergreen with them.

Barbara cleared her throat as she came back in the room with Zoe. "Careful, you two."

Allie and Ryan spun around.

Barbara snickered and pointed above their heads. "You're standing under the mistletoe."

They both tilted their chins up, and then practically belly-bumped trying to get out from under it in a hurry.

"Oh! That's…" Allie moved a giant step to the right. "I. Oh, dear."

"Oops." Ryan looked like a trapped rabbit.

"I…uh…I should go," Allie rambled. "Have a good night." She raced for the door, snagging her coat on the way…but part of her wanted to know what that kiss would have been like.

"You too," he called after her.

Allie was thankful for the direct path to the exit. The huge wreath slapped against the heavy wooden door, sending a waft of snow drifting to the welcome mat below.

She stood there, taking in deep breaths of cold air as the snow fell around her.

What was that in there? She fanned herself. *If we'd kissed under the mistletoe...N*o. She couldn't allow herself to think about that. She walked carefully on the icy sidewalk back to her truck.

Just as she got behind the wheel, her phone rang.

It was Spencer. She took in a deep breath, then sent the call to voice mail. She couldn't talk to him right now.

Chapter Fourteen

Allie pulled into her driveway. The outside of her house wasn't decorated anywhere near as grandly as Barbara's Country Inn this year, since she'd planned on being out of town, but she was glad she'd at least put up the garland and white lights.

Dragging her bags up the stairs, she let out a sigh as she dropped them right there in the entry hall. She wasn't normally one to leave things lying around, but there was no sense unpacking since her flight would leave tomorrow. Hopefully.

Too tired to sleep, she started a pot of tea and then sat in her favorite chair, hugging the throw pillow against her chest. Even if the day hadn't gone according to plan, it had been fun hanging out with Ryan and Zoe.

Her living room was decorated for the holidays. Not as much as she'd usually do, but she hadn't been able to resist. It would've felt a little sad and lonely to come home tonight to a house full of boxes. At least the decorations made it feel lived in and cheerful.

A knock came from the door, and for a fleeting moment, she hoped it might be Ryan. She ran her fingers through her hair and jumped up, and then realized how crazy that was. Ryan didn't even know where she lived. She slowed down and opened the door. "Mom?"

"Hey, darling." Carol balanced a dinner plate in her hands.

"Come on in." Allie stepped aside so she could enter. "You didn't have to bring me food." Although, on second glance, she was glad she had. It was all of her favorites. Sliced turkey, greens, and mashed potatoes and gravy. Dad made the best mashed potatoes and gravy in the world.

"I'm your mother. Of course I did."

Allie put the plate on the counter, then turned and poured two mugs of tea. She handed one to her mom.

Mom walked into the dining room, then stopped. "And why did you put up all your Christmas decorations if you aren't even going to be here?"

She held the warm mug close to her body. "I know it. I couldn't help myself, but at least I didn't put up a tree. I'm not completely Christmas crazy."

"Just a *little* Christmas crazy." Mom held her fingers up with about a half-inch space, then an inch.

"Exactly," Allie said.

"Did you get Ryan and Zoe settled?"

"Yes. They're at the inn."

Carol took a sip of her tea. "He seems like a good guy."

"He does. Yeah." Allie toyed with the tea tag

hanging over the edge of her mug. "He's a doctor and a single dad. I don't know how he does it."

Carol's brow arched. "So...have you talked to Spencer?"

"Everything's fine." She really didn't want to discuss Spencer.

"Honey, as long as you feel like you are doing the best thing for you, then I'm on board."

"I do." Mom must have sensed Allie's hesitation. It was a relief to hear her say that. "Thank you."

"It's just not going to be the same without you around here." Carol fidgeted. "I think that's partly why your dad and I are talking about retiring."

"You are?" Allie's heart sped up. That was the last thing she'd expected to hear come from her mother's mouth. The Chris Kringle Kitchen was the heartbeat of Evergreen. She'd assumed it always would be. Plus, she couldn't imagine Mom and Dad with nothing to do. They loved running the diner.

"Actually, your father is doing most of the talking, and I am listening politely."

"You don't want to do it?" *Of course not. Evergreen is home.*

"I can't imagine leaving Evergreen. But if my brave daughter can start a new chapter in her life, then I guess her parents can, too."

Wow. Not only retiring, but possibly moving? She couldn't even picture it.

Mom lifted her mug, and Allie touched her own mug to it, hoping for the best.

"But don't tell anyone," Mom said. "Especially Ezra. I don't think his heart could take it."

"I don't think so, either." Allie shared the laugh with Mom. Ezra was taking his new role as Mayor of Evergreen very seriously, and any change as a personal attack. Too bad the man wasn't as easygoing as his dad had been. Everyone loved the older Mayor Green.

Carol took another sip of tea, then checked her watch. "Oh, I'd better get going. I'm going to be late." She set her mug down.

"Where are you off to?"

"To spread a little Christmas cheer." Carol pulled her hands to her hips. "You know, I think maybe we'll stop by the inn for Zoe and Ryan."

Allie perked up. She knew exactly how Mom was going to spread cheer tonight. It was an Evergreen tradition, and Allie wanted to join in the fun and surprise them, too. "Well, I want a little cheer. Can't I tag along?" She pretended to pout.

"Yes, you can tag along," Carol teased. "Go get your coat." She blew her a kiss and headed outside to get the car started.

"Great." Allie put on her coat and wrapped her scarf around her neck. She hurried out the front door and excitement pushed her into a run. She jumped in the SUV, and they headed off to pick up the others. She couldn't wait to see Zoe and Ryan's faces when they opened the door. She imagined the way his eyes would sparkle, crinkling just at the edges when he smiled like they had earlier today. A genuine smile. One that made her feel like smiling, too.

Ryan and Zoe put their things in the guest room, then went back downstairs to hang out in the living room in front of the fireplace. Barbara had served them a tray of those fresh cookies they'd smelled when they'd come in, along with ice-cold milk. "There are games over on the shelf." They decided to play cards.

Sitting in the floor at the coffee table, Ryan eyed the cards in his hand. "Do you have any sevens?"

Zoe set down her glass of milk. "Go fish."

"Ugh. Again?" He took a card from the stack, adding it to his ever-growing hand.

"I'm just that good," Zoe said with a smug smile, then perked up as a sound came from the front yard.

Barbara walked into the living room. "What is that?" With a tilt of her head, she went to the front door. Ryan folded his cards and laid them down on the table, and then he and Zoe followed behind Barbara to investigate.

Barbara opened the door, and the sound grew into a harmonious round of "Deck the Halls." "Oh! Look!"

Seven carolers held candles in front of them as they belted out the joyous song amid the freezing temperatures and snowflakes. Ryan stepped behind Zoe, placing his hands on her shoulders.

Right in the center of them, Allie stood, bundled

in her red coat, singing, "Toll the ancient Yule-tide carol. Fa-la-la-la-la, la-la-la-la."

"Merry Christmas," the carolers exclaimed.

Barbara held her hand to her heart, and Zoe flashed him her thousand-watt smile.

His whole life, he'd never had someone Christmas carol his house. What a glorious feeling it inspired.

The group began to leave. Allie turned back around and waved to them.

His heart pounded.

She and her mom caught up with the others on the street. It looked like they were heading next door.

It was hard to take his eyes off Allie. He liked the way her smile lit up her whole face. He couldn't even see her without smiling, too. She was contagious. In a really good way.

Barbara closed the door, and the three of them went back into the living room. "That was so special," she said.

"It was." He couldn't believe how much joy that had brought him. "Come on, Zoe. Let me beat you at cards."

"That'll never happen," she said, dropping down to the ground and playing the next hand.

Zoe couldn't quit talking about the carolers between rounds of *Go Fish,* at which she beat him again quite handily.

They turned in early, optimistic the flights would be back on schedule soon.

The next morning, the snow had finally stopped, and the sun was bright. Ryan checked his phone for an update on the airport. Luckily, the news was good.

He went downstairs, where Zoe was already working on a plate of bacon and eggs that Barbara had cooked to order for her. "Would you mind if Zoe stayed with you while I walk down to the diner?" Ryan asked.

"Of course," Barbara said.

Zoe nodded. "I'll be fine here."

"Great. I'll be back shortly."

Barbara piped up. "To the right out of the front gate. Two blocks, and you're there."

"Thank you." He got his coat and walked outside. The sun took the sharpness from the air, making it a pretty comfortable stroll down Main Street.

When he got to the Chris Kringle Kitchen, the *Sorry, We're Closed* sign was still in the window, but the lights were on. He tapped on the glass of the window and walked inside. Allie was sitting at a table with her mom and another woman.

"Hi, Allie," Ryan said.

"Ryan, hi." She got up. Watching her walk toward him, he suddenly felt like a teenager. Nervous and awkward. "Where's Zoe?"

"She's back at the inn with Barbara. I heard the airport is open again, so I thought I'd come and see if we could hitch a ride back with you."

"Of course," Allie said.

"Great."

"Oh, Ryan, I want you to meet my friend Michelle Lansing."

Michelle waved from where she was sitting next to Carol helping her top off the salt and pepper shakers. "Hi."

"Hi, Michelle."

"And I think you've met my mom and dad."

Joe stopped wiping down the glass bakery case. "Hi."

"Nice to see you." He gave Carol a wave. "Hi again."

"This is Dr. Ryan Bellamy."

A man who'd just come in the front door inserted himself into the conversation. "Doctor?" Ryan swung around toward the newcomer.

"And this is Mayor Ezra Green," Allie said.

"You're a doctor?" Ezra moved forward with his hand extended.

He shook his hand. "I am. Yes."

Ezra didn't let go, instead, placing his hand on top of theirs. "You know, our town doctor just retired and—"

"Leave him alone, Ezra." Allie placed a protective hand on Ryan's arm. Ryan laughed nervously.

"Right. Sorry." He clapped his hands together. "Listen up, everybody. I have some bad news. They had to shut down the highway."

"What? Why?" Allie looked to Ryan.

"The storm last night caused a rock slide."

"I don't believe this," Allie said.

"Why is that a problem?" Ryan asked.

She hated to be the one to break the news to him. "There's only one road in and out of town."

"And now it's blocked by a bunch of big rocks," Ezra said.

How could this even be possible? "Well, when will it open?" he asked.

"Tomorrow, maybe..." Ezra didn't look confident at all.

"Tomorrow?" Ryan repeated. "We're going to miss our flight."

"Yeah." Allie chewed on her lip.

"Well, there must be some other way out of town." Ryan grappled for ideas. "Snowmobiles? Snowplow? A helicopter?"

"Forget about getting out, what about people getting in?" Michelle threw her hands in the air. "Nobody will be able to come to the Christmas Festival."

"This is terrible," Joe agreed.

"Everyone in Evergreen can come," Carol said.

"But I've got people coming from Montpelier, Burlington..." Michelle jumped to her feet. "Allie? What are we going to do?"

"All right. All right. Why don't we meet at Henry's barn this afternoon and start setting up for the festival? If the road gets cleared, then great. If it doesn't, then this year, the festival will be just for Evergreen...and guests." She gestured to Ryan with a sweet smile.

Michelle calmed down. "Okay. Well, I guess I feel better."

"You know," Ezra said. "I think this is another situation that could've been solved if we had an app."

"Ezra, please!" Michelle stood, turned her back on him, and walked away.

"This is a good idea," Ezra insisted as he tracked Michelle to the other side of the diner.

Ryan pulled his hands to his neck. He closed his eyes and let out a sigh.

Allie stepped closer to him. "Hey. I'm so sorry. If I hadn't invited you here, you wouldn't be stuck."

His gut twisted. How could this be happening? But it wasn't her fault. She was the best part of everything that had gone wrong. In an attempt to lighten his disappointment, he said, "You didn't cause the rockslide." Ryan tilted his head playfully. "Did you?"

"No, I didn't," Allie said thoughtfully. "My neighbor has my jackhammer."

He sighed. "I just really wanted this Christmas to be better…"

"Well, y'all are stuck here another day," she said. "Maybe I could help make Christmas a little better." She held his gaze. "For Zoe."

Were they still talking about Zoe?

"We do have plenty of snow." she continued.

Where was she going with this?

"I have some ideas. Are you game?" she asked.

How could anyone say no to that smile of hers? It was infectious. "I'm game."

"Excellent." She held up one finger then turned

and ran over to her mom. "I'm going to help Ryan salvage the day for Zoe. I'll see you all later."

"Wait!" Dad dipped into the kitchen and then reappeared in a snap, carrying a white bakery box. "Here. Take these with you."

She opened the box. "Christmas cookies. Thank you."

"Can't have a Christmas play day without cookies."

"Thanks, Dad." She walked over to Ryan. "Come on. We have to stop by my house on the way to the inn."

Ryan waved goodbye and followed Allie out to the street. "You are one bundle of energy," he said to her.

She balanced the box of cookies in the palm of one hand and carried it like a waitress tray, then held her arms out, letting the snowflakes land on her coat. "It's Christmas. I love Christmas."

"I see that." Was she always this joyful? She made Christmas fun again, and that wasn't something he'd expected to feel for a very long time.

"My house is at the end of this block. The blue one. I'll race you." She took off down the street, getting a head start.

"Hey, wait." Ryan took off, catching up to her in just a couple long strides. He tagged her as he passed and turned up the driveway toward the pretty blue Cape Cod-style house. He leaned forward, huffing and puffing. "Okay, I might be a little out of shape."

"You beat me!"

"Yes, I did." He raised his hand for a high five.

She slapped his hand, her fingers brushing against his, sending an unexpected tingle up his arm. She walked up to the garage door and lifted it.

It had to be twenty degrees warmer in here just getting out of the wind. "What are we looking for?" He noticed right off how organized her garage was. Sports equipment in one area, tools in another. Storage boxes neatly stacked and labeled in perfect block letters. Not a doctor's handwriting. He had typical doctor chicken scratch. Always had. Maybe doctors of veterinarian medicine didn't fall into the pitiful handwriting category.

"Not *looking* for anything. I know exactly where it is." She headed to the far right corner of the garage. On the third shelf sat a bright red box labeled *Frosty*.

"Frosty?" Ryan wasn't quite sure what to expect from that. "What do you have in there? A melted snowman? We're not resuscitating a snowman, are we?"

"Real funny, Doc." She gave him a playful sideways glance.

"Good, because I'm pretty sure defibrillators and melted snow are not a good mix."

"True," Allie said. "But no." She tapped the box. "I was going to show you what's in this box, but now you're going to have to wait and see."

"Oh, I see how you are." The lighthearted banter was unexpected, leaving him a little off balance but enjoying every moment of it.

She carried the big box against her stomach. She

pulled the garage door back down, and they walked to the inn.

Zoe came running out as soon as they got to the sidewalk. "Hi, Allie. Dad! Is Allie driving us to the airport?"

"Not today," he said.

"What?" Zoe looked confused. "Are we staying?"

"For at least another day," Ryan said, and no sooner did he get the words out of his mouth than Zoe leaped into his arms. "Awesome!"

"Are you up for a fun day? Evergreen style?" Allie raised the box in the air.

"Yes!" Zoe jumped to the ground. "What are we going to do?"

Barbara peeked around the front door. "Everything okay out here?"

"Actually, I have a favor to ask." Allie walked over to the porch. "Do you mind if we build you a snowman?"

"I'd love that," Barbara said. "Absolutely! Oh, wait. Zoe, let me get you a hat. You'll freeze out there with no hat on." Barbara ran inside, then came back with a red toboggan and gloves for Zoe.

"Thank you, Barbara."

Allie gave Zoe a hug around the shoulders. "Great. I've got all the stuff to make the best snowman ever… right here in this box." She squatted down on the porch and took off the lid. One by one she began taking things out. "A top hat!" She popped it on her head and made a goofy face, then handed it to Zoe, who did the same thing. "And we've got a scarf, and matching gloves. Two sticks for arms. Coal buttons and a—"

"You have a carrot in that box?" Ryan asked smugly.

"Well, it's a wooden carrot, but it works."

"You are very prepared."

"Have to be. It's part of the Evergreen Code of Christmas Conduct."

"How big of a snowman are we going to build?" Zoe asked.

"Big! Big enough to wear this top hat."

"Big as you?"

"Sure. Let's get started."

Ryan plopped down in the snow and started pulling snow toward him like a human excavator. In a matter of minutes, he had a huge base started. Allie and Zoe joined forces on the middle one. Packing and rolling, they built the icy ball up to a generous size.

"Ready to stack that one?" he asked, trudging through the snow toward them.

"I think so," Zoe said.

Ryan and Allie rolled the medium snowball over to the big bottom and then lifted it on top. They gave it a good twist and pat to wedge them together so they wouldn't fall apart.

"What do you think so far?" Allie posed in front of it.

"It's the headless snowman," Zoe teased. "I'll start making the head." When she had a snowball the size of a big hug, she asked her dad to do the honors.

"It's perfect!" Zoe ran over and grabbed the top hat. "Put on his hat and scarf!"

"It's looking good," Allie said.

"You do the face," Zoe said.

Allie grabbed all the fake coal buttons and started placing them on the snowman: two for eyes, and five in a curving row as the mouth. She twisted the wooden carrot into the middle of the face. Ryan put the sticks in for the arms and then lifted Zoe onto his back to put the gloves on them.

"Frosty!" Zoe skipped in a circle around him. The snowman was a good few inches taller than Allie. Probably five-feet-six, if Ryan had to guess.

"Awesome," Allie said, digging into her pocket for her phone. "I've got to get a picture."

Ryan and Zoe mugged for the camera with Frosty.

"All right. Ready?"

Ryan jumped in the air, and Zoe lunged in front.

"Another pose," Allie cheered them on. "One. Two. Three."

They both did a leaping high five.

"Selfie!" Allie ran to get in front of the snowman, extending her arm out as far as she could. "Scoot in," she instructed. "Say 'Frosty!'"

"Frosty!" they all yelled.

Allie then held up her fingers in a peace sign as she blew a kiss, while Zoe clapped the snowman's hand, and Ryan photo bombed them right before he stole the top hat and plopped it right down on Zoe's head.

Zoe giggled out of control.

"I want a picture in the hat, too," Allie said.

"Here. Let me take the next picture." He grabbed the camera, and Allie danced around the snowman with the top hat as Ryan snapped photos.

Allie grabbed the camera from Ryan and took a close-up of him. Her phone played a tune. "Oh, wait! I'm getting a call." She glanced at the phone, then looked up with a half smile, raising a finger in the air. "I'll be right back." She stepped away.

"Come on, Zoe," he said. "This will be fun."

Allie tucked herself off to the side, out of the wind, next to the large nannyberry bushes. "Hi." She held her hand over her other ear so she could hear better.

"Hey. Are you at the airport?" Spencer asked.

"No." Allie hated to give him more bad news. "The storm last night shut down the highway. I'm going to be here another day…at least."

He cleared his throat. "Why didn't you stay in Burlington?"

He was mad, but she didn't have any other options. "All the hotels were booked. I would've had to sleep in the truck."

"Okay." Spencer sighed. "So, what's the plan?"

"Well…" She watched Ryan and Zoe and the fun they were having in the snow. Without knowing when the roads would open, her time in DC was getting squeezed. "I'm thinking at this point it might make more sense for me to stay here."

"Allie, what about Christmas?"

"Spencer, my folks are talking about retiring. This could be my last Christmas in Evergreen." It might have been anyway, but now it seemed even more important.

"I mean..." Spencer's voice was tight. "I was just really looking forward to spending it with you is all."

"I know. Me too. But I'll be there after Christmas, and we can have plenty of time then."

He didn't say anything.

"Okay?" Allie asked.

"Okay," he said.

"I'll call you tomorrow."

"Bye."

Allie put the phone in her pocket. He sounded so disappointed. Had she made the right decision? It wasn't like she could change anything right now, anyway. Until the road opened back up, there were no other options.

She walked back over to where she'd left Ryan and Zoe and saw them both sprawled out in the snow making snow angels. Her heart took an instant leap for the better.

"Allie!" Zoe's arms and legs scissored like they were motorized.

"Hey. Look at you guys!" Allie drew closer.

"We're making snow angels!"

"They're gorgeous," Allie said.

Ryan sat up and then his face twisted. "Mine looks more like a snow gorilla."

Allie put on a serious expression. "A Christmas gorilla."

That made Zoe giggle. "It's so much fun here." Zoe slapped the soft snow from her gloves. "We should do something nice for Barbara. She's been so nice to us."

Ryan turned to Zoe, looking proud of her. "That's really sweet."

"I've got an idea," Allie said.

He gave her that *I-bet-you-do* look.

Well, he'd just have to wait and see.

Chapter Fifteen

Ryan looked at Allie with interest as they hiked down to her house to get her truck. How was it that he felt this comfortable around someone he'd met by accident after a brief interaction? She'd not only made sure they had a place to stay, but had made the stay extra special by sharing her traditions with them. It was like they'd known each other forever. And her interactions with Zoe were just as easy.

It was true her trip was cancelled too, but her family was here. She had plenty of other things to do besides spend her time with them, but he was thankful that she was.

"So, what is this big idea you have?" he asked when they got to her house.

"We're going Christmas tree shopping." Allie started the truck, and they all buckled up.

"Are we going to the tree farm near Henry's farm? Near Snowflake?"

Allie shook her head. "No, they're closed at this time of night, but there's a nice tree lot right here in town. We'll find a very pretty tree there. Plus, the proceeds go to help with school programs for our students here in Evergreen. A win-win."

"That's nice," Ryan said.

Allie drove up the road, making a couple of turns, then pulled into the parking lot of the grocery store. Off to the far right in an empty lot, there was an old Airstream motorhome parked next to a well-lit area filled with Christmas trees. There were still quite a few to pick from this close to the holiday.

"I think Dad and I should pick out the tree," Zoe said. "I mean, you already said you pick out the scrawny ones, and Barbara deserves a big, pretty tree for her living room."

"Awww. Scrawny trees need love, too," Allie said as she climbed out of the truck.

But Ryan was in full agreement with Zoe. "I agree, Zoe. How about something like this one?" He walked straight over to a conical-shaped tree.

Zoe curled her lip. "That one is too skinny." She ran over to a super-tall tree that had a blue ribbon tied to its top branch. "This one?"

Ryan shook his head. "That one is way too tall. We'd have to cut three feet from the bottom of it just to get it in the door."

Zoe put her finger to her lip. "That wouldn't be good."

Allie clapped her hands to get their attention and thumbed toward a small tree to her right.

Both Ryan and Zoe said, "No!"

"Fine." Allie stroked the top branch of the pitiful little tree.

Zoe skipped between the rows of trees. "I think this is the one, Dad." Zoe had sidled up to a full tree that rose to about seven feet tall.

As he got closer, the aroma put him in a holiday mood. The shape of this tree was ideal, too. Wide at the bottom with a perfect taper. The trunk was straight all the way to the top, where the angel or star would shine. "I think you're right," Ryan agreed.

"What do you think, Allie?" Zoe looked hopeful.

"Thanks for asking." She gave the scrawny little three-foot tree an apologetic nod, then started laughing. "It's beautiful. I think Barbara will love it too."

"Perfect!"

The lot attendant walked over. "Did you decide on a tree already?"

"We did," Zoe spoke for the group.

The tree lot guy seemed impressed, giving Ryan a high five as he called one of his helpers over to cut the tree from the post. The helper shook out the loose needles and leaves, then wrapped it and put it in the back of Allie's truck. Ryan pulled out his wallet and paid the man.

The lot attendant checked the tree to make sure it wouldn't fly out of the back on the ride home, and then closed the tailgate. "All set."

"Thanks!" They climbed into the truck. It started right up, thanks to her lucky charm passengers. She might need them to ride shotgun more often. Allie fiddled with the radio to find some Christmas music. As if special ordered, the next song that played was "O Christmas Tree."

Zoe was so excited on the short trip back that she never did even turn around and sit right in the seat. "Barbara is going to love this tree."

"She's going to be so surprised." Allie pulled her truck into the driveway at Barbara's Country Inn, trying to get as close as possible to the front door.

They got out of the truck, and Allie dropped the back tailgate with a thud, hoping the loud clunk hadn't roused Barbara all the way inside the house. They waited a minute, but after a moment, it was apparent they hadn't spoiled the surprise. Thank goodness. With no sign of Barbara, they got to work.

"This is going to be great!" Zoe danced around the side of the truck.

"It was a very thoughtful idea." Ryan smiled at Allie. "Both of you." He wrestled with the huge tree.

"Let's get this inside," Allie said. "I'll help."

"Me too," said Zoe.

Ryan slid the tree out of the bed of the truck and then set it on its trunk. He lowered it horizontally, positioning himself at the heavy trunk end. "Allie, you can grab the middle, and Zoe, you can balance the top." They got into position and marched to the front door.

"Left. Left. Left-right-left," Zoe chanted.

At the porch, Ryan stopped and let the trunk rest on the ground. "Zoe, you'll have to get the door."

"No problem." Zoe twisted the doorknob and gave it a push. "Surprise!"

"Ho. Ho. Ho," Allie called out as they breezed in with the tree in tow.

The fireplace mantel was already decorated with tall glass hurricane shades filled with shiny silver ornaments. Barbara was in the middle of pinning hand-crafted stockings to it now. The fire burned brightly with dancing orange, yellow, and blue flames. The blast of warmth thawed them as they stood there holding the tree.

Barbara turned around. "What's this?"

"Well, we figured since we have to impose on you for one more night, the least we could do is get you a Christmas tree." He stood the tree up in the room. It was the perfect height.

"You didn't have to do that!" She rushed over to get a closer look. "But I'm glad you did."

"Can we decorate it?" Zoe asked.

"Of course," Barbara said. "Let's go get some ornaments." She took Zoe by the hand and disappeared into another room.

Ryan peered around the tree to Allie. "Shall we trim it up?"

"Let's do it."

"Okay." He took the tree in a big bear hug and toted it to the corner of the room that had been cleared all except for a chair. "Looks like this is where she planned to put it." He balanced the tree and had Allie hold it while he moved the chair out of the way.

Barbara came back in, carrying the large red-and-green tree stand. "That's perfect. I brought the stand."

"Great," Ryan said. "Drop it right there. Allie and I can get her secured."

"Thanks," Barbara said. "We're gathering the ornaments." She left as quickly as she'd arrived.

Allie open and closed her hands. "That tree is sappy."

"It's fresh. Do you know that's the first time I've ever bought a fresh tree?"

"No way. Really?"

"Yep." He positioned the tree in the stand. "I guess out of convenience. We always had artificial ones. This has been an amazing day." He was laser-focused on making Zoe's Christmas the best possible, and yet, here he was, experiencing new things and having more fun than he'd had in a very long time. And with a complete stranger.

"It has," she enthused, then her expression softened. "So great."

He swallowed hard. "Um. Is the tree straight?"

"Oh. Yeah. Hang on." She backed up. "A little more to the right. Yes! That's perfect."

Zoe and Barbara came in carrying boxes.

"Are there lights in any of those?" Allie asked.

"I hope so," Barbara said. "There should be."

"We can put those on while you all are gathering

the rest of the ornaments," Ryan offered, then stoked the fire to keep it going.

"I won't argue with that. The lights are the hardest part." Barbara lifted the lid off the tall box. "And here they are."

"I love these old-style lights." Allie pulled out the top strand. The green cord separated the large white bulbs. She plugged one end into the receptacle nearby, and it came to life. "Got one!"

Zoe and Barbara clapped, then headed out of the room to retrieve the rest of the ornaments.

Ryan pulled out strands, trying to keep them from tangling, plugging each strand into the outlet one at a time to test them. Only one strand was a dud, and they seemed to have plenty of lights to fill the tree without it. He wrapped the lights around his elbow and palm in a nice, organized roll.

"Start at the top," Allie said, tiptoeing and reaching as high as she could.

He didn't even need a ladder. He draped the lights around the uppermost branches until he got down to where she could reach.

He handed the coil of lights to her, and she draped and pushed them deep into the branches, securing them along the way. She got around her side and then passed the lights back to him; their hands touched as they wrangled the tangle of lights back and forth. They continued until they got all the way to the bottom.

"Let's plug them in and see how we did," Allie said. He plugged the end into the wall.

Allie gasped. "This is the fastest I've ever been able to put up lights. And they're perfect."

"I'm kind of an old pro."

"You must be."

He touched her arm. Her skin was soft and warm. He crouched to her height. "I always say you have to put the squint test on it to be sure you have enough lights and no gaps."

Her giggle sounded nervous, but she followed along. "Really?"

"Yes, really," he said. "Face the tree. Now squint your eyes. You shouldn't see any big gaps."

"Oh my gosh. You're right. It does work. There's one little spot right…"

"Here," he said. "I noticed that too." He reached between the branches and repositioned a few of the lights.

Allie squinted, squinching her face. "That's it!"

"It is," Barbara echoed. "How did you do that so fast? It's beautiful even without the ornaments."

Zoe shook her head. "Oh, no. We need the ornaments." She put one of the boxes down on the floor next to the tree and started trimming the tree. "These are so pretty, Barbara. I've never seen ornaments like this."

"That's because many of these are older than you. Older than me even," Barbara said. "My parents bought them in Germany. My daddy was in the army over there. They are very delicate. I always end up breaking a couple each year and it makes me so sad, but now I save all the broken pieces and put the pretty colored glass into those clear ornaments to hang on to the memories."

"That's a neat tradition," Zoe said. "Dad, we need some traditions."

She was right. And being here, they'd just shared a ton of new ones. It was more than just the holiday. It was the community, and sharing. "Traditions are good. I think trimming a tree with friends three days before Christmas is a pretty good one." Ryan hung a glitzy magenta, turquoise and white ball high on one of the top branches.

Allie nodded. "It is."

"We're a good team." He liked the way her eyes twinkled.

"We are," she said.

Barbara carried two boxes of ornaments, and Zoe tagged along, carrying homemade strands of cranberries and popcorn. "More to come," Barbara said as they put everything on the coffee table.

"Thanks," Allie said, picking up a strand of popcorn garland. "So how's that 'stay as far away from Christmas as possible' strategy working for you?"

"Really well. Clearly," he said with a chuckle. He grabbed the other end of the popcorn garland and helped Allie drape it around the center of the tree. "I'll tell you. There's something about this place that makes it tough to resist the Christmas spirit."

"Evergreen will do that to you. I decorated my place this year. And I'm not even going to be here." She dropped the garland to her waist and turned her attention back to Ryan. "Oh. Actually it's a good thing I did."

"What do you mean?"

"It turns out I don't think I'm going to DC for Christmas this year."

"Why not?"

Allie gathered another strand of garland. This one made of paper loops. "It's complicated."

"Hmm." That sounded serious.

"A boy," she said, blushing slightly.

Ryan felt more disappointed than he'd expected, although he'd been wondering. "Oh." He tried to play it off.

Allie laughed. "Spencer. Two years of long distance and a relationship that just couldn't handle the distance part, but we were going to spend this Christmas together and just sort of see if there was something there…"

"No. I get it," he said. "Sarah and I were long distance when we started. I was in Boston, and she was in this little town in Ohio."

"And that worked out well though, right?"

"Yes. I guess we just knew we'd wind up together, so it helped us get through it."

He wondered what she was thinking right now.

"I actually considered going there and becoming a small town doctor." He looked at Zoe. She seemed to like that idea. "Now, I kind of wish I had. My job doesn't allow the kind of time I'd like to spend with Zoe. Which is hard."

Why am I telling her all of this? He'd never shared this much with anyone since Sarah died. There was something so easy about being with Allie, and somehow sharing this with her made him feel like he wasn't alone anymore.

"Don't tell Mayor Ezra that." She eyed him playfully. "He'll open up an office for you in Town Hall."

"Doc Bellamy. It's got a good ring."

"Yeah. It does." She waved a hand in the air. "Dr. B. The doctor is in."

He could imagine living here. Him treating the townsfolk, and her taking care of their pets. "I gotta say. This is the last place I thought I'd find myself three days before Christmas." *With someone like you. Laughing, and having fun.*

"Same here."

"But...I guess it's not so bad." He handed her a piece of popcorn that had fallen from the garland.

"No." She shook her head. She held his gaze, her bright blue eyes wide, giving him her full attention. Her voice held more than just the words. "Not bad at all."

At that moment, he felt more alive than he had all year.

"You guys ready?" Barbara and Zoe carried two more boxes into the room. "Here are the ornaments."

"Come on," said Zoe. "Let's decorate the tree."

"Yes. Let's." Barbara hung the first ornament: a shiny red beaded box with a ribbon made of golden rings on top. Zoe placed a golden pinecone next, and then they all chipped in to adorn the tree. Ryan, Barbara, and Zoe hung ornaments, and Allie started tucking big silk poinsettias between the branches. It made the tree look so fancy. Like one of those department store trees. They were done before the fire even needed stoking again.

Zoe beamed as brightly as the lights on the tree. "This is, like…the best tree ever."

"I agree," Barbara said. "I bet the one at the festival won't be anywhere near as nice."

"We'll see when we go to the barn later tonight." Allie sat on the floor at the coffee table, straightening the angel's dress. The flaxen-haired figure was dressed in all white. Her wings were made of soft fluffy feathers, and delicate beads, pearls and crystals shimmered on her long gown. Her hands were hidden in a furry muff, protected from the Vermont winter night.

Zoe sat down next to her. "Is there a Christmas festival where you're moving, Allie?"

"I think there is, but it's nothing like this one in Evergreen."

"Then why would you want to move there?"

Ryan loved the innocence of Zoe's remarks.

Allie glanced his way. "Well, I've lived here my whole life and it's a wonderful place, it really is, but there's a whole big world out there. I want to see it. I'm ready for a change. My grandpa used to say, the further away you get from where you started, the closer you get to where you belong."

Lines creased in Zoe's forehead. "But what if you belong here?"

Ryan watched Allie. She didn't have a response to that.

"Okay, I think we are ready for the angel," Barbara said. "Who wants to do the honors?"

"Me, please!" Zoe threw her hand in the air. Allie handed her the pretty angel tree topper.

"Go for it, Zoe." Barbara stepped back to watch.

"Here we go!" Ryan lifted her up and balanced her on his shoulders. Zoe reached forward, stretching to reach the tallest branch. She set the angel on top.

It was perfect. Mere inches from the ceiling. Ryan set Zoe back down.

Barbara walked back over to the light switch. "Everybody ready?" With a flip of the switch, the lights in the room went dark.

"Drum roll." Allie started patting her thighs with her hands, and Zoe and Ryan joined in. Barbara plugged the tree lights back in, and they all cheered at the glorious sight.

Ryan hugged Zoe. This was more than he could have ever hoped for her tonight.

Allie and Barbara hugged, then Barbara fussed with a few of the lights to get it just right.

"You all have been such a Christmas blessing to me," Barbara said. "Thank you. I have a wonderful pot roast ready. Allie, won't you stay and have dinner with us?"

"I'd love to."

Zoe did the honors of saying grace, and following the amen, they all dug right into the warm meal, then helped Barbara clear the dishes.

"I'm going to head over to the barn and see how I can help with the festival. Anyone else up to going?" Allie looked hopeful.

"I'm in," Ryan said.

"Me too." Zoe put the last of the dishes on the counter. "I hope we get to decorate another tree. That was fun."

Chapter Sixteen

Allie drove Ryan and Zoe over to Henry's barn to see how they could help out with getting ready for the Christmas Festival tonight. The place buzzed with activity. Townsfolk were setting up tents outside of the barn, and through the open barn doors they could see booths and a stage inside.

"It looks so different," Zoe said.

A wreath that had to be every bit of seven feet tall had been propped up on bales of straw to the left of the tall sliding barn doors, and strands of white bulbs ran from the hay door at the top of the barn all the way to the outbuilding across the dirt lane. There was an aura of joy there tonight.

All the greenery against the shiny red building looked perfectly Christmas-y. Inside the barn, someone had dropped lengths of shiny fabric from the rafters, with extra-large ball and star ornaments dangling from them. It was beautiful, and they weren't even nearly done yet.

Allie, Ryan, and Zoe walked up as the children's

choir started to rehearse "We Wish You A Merry Christmas" inside the barn. Hannah stood in front of eleven youngsters on the makeshift stage. The kids ranged in age from seven to fifteen. Hannah led them in song like a real choir conductor, her arms carving the air, her hand closing as if pulling taffy, leading the children in perfect harmony and a high-energy celebration of the season.

Along one side of the barn there was a hot cocoa and eggnog booth, and a Pin the Nose on the Reindeer station filled the space next to that. Allie's mom stacked cute polar bears wearing red-and-green scarves in the prize shack. Kids would go crazy to win one of those. Dads had better have been practicing their throwing skills.

Old barrels served as tables for guests to nosh and mingle, and small Christmas trees were sitting on big wrapped presents that helped divide the space by themes. Food. Crafts. Games. Entertainment.

"Whoaaaa." Zoe tipped her chin to the ceiling, turning around trying to take it all in.

"Look at all this," Allie said. Even though she'd run this festival for years, she was impressed with all the town had accomplished. Henry's barn was the perfect setting for this year's festival.

"Wow," was all Ryan could say.

Allie applauded as Hannah gave the final cue for the choir to finish on the last note. As Hannah high-fived each of her singers, Zoe turned to her dad. "Hey, Dad? Can I be in the choir?"

"That's for the festival, kiddo. We're not going to be here, remember?" He squeezed her shoulder.

A pout settled on Zoe's face as she turned away.

"Zoe!" Carol called from over at the cocoa booth. "Merry Christmas." She held a large Christmas bear, clapping his paws.

Zoe ran over to Carol, and Ryan followed. Allie noticed Michelle zipping across the barn wearing a pretty white sweater and red scarf. She couldn't wait to tell her how great a job she was doing, but then she noticed Ezra was nipping at Michelle's heels, complaining about where the craft booths should be. Michelle was probably about ready to lock Ezra in one of those booths and throw away the key.

Allie couldn't help but eavesdrop.

Michelle threw her hands in the air. "Ezra! You are making me crazy. I am in charge of the festival. Me, not you."

"The festival is an important part of the town and *I* am the mayor of the town," Ezra said pointing to himself. "Me, not you."

Michelle grimaced. "Your daddy retired, and nobody else wanted the job."

Allie cringed. *That was a low blow.*

Ezra shrugged it off. "A win is still a win."

"Ezra, I've got this under control. Okay? There are no problems." Her phone rang. With a huff, she answered it. "Hello? Right. Okay. Got it." She disconnected the call and all of her bravado was gone. She suddenly looked like one of those big yard inflatables that had lost power. "Okay, now we've got a problem," Michelle shouted.

"I knew it!" Ezra propped his hands on his hips.

Allie couldn't stand by listening to this. "Wait. What? What's the problem?"

"We're not going to have any food for the festival." Michelle swept at her bangs.

"What?" Ezra's eyes bugged.

"Mrs. Wallace and the ladies from the church are usually in charge of the feast and the cookies, but they went to Montpelier yesterday for a book club and now..."

Carol finished the sentence. "Now they can't get back because the road is closed."

"Right. And even if it got fixed tomorrow, they're not going to have enough time to prepare everything we need." Michelle's hands balled into fists.

"There's got to be something we can do." Allie glanced around the room, hoping for a solution. "Hold on a second. I got an idea." She walked to the center of the barn and stood on a stack of hay bales. She cupped her hands around her mouth. "Excuse me, everyone. May I have your attention please?" She raised her hand high in the air hoping others would follow. "Raise your hand if you like to bake."

People started raising their hands. First just a couple, then several.

"Great," Allie said, relieved. "Anyone else?"

Just about everyone had a hand in the air.

Allie sighed with relief. "Great. We need your help.

If we all bake something, we will have plenty of food for the festival. Can everyone help?"

Heads were nodding.

"Mom, can you get a list of what people are making? Anything goes, but we will need a couple of specific things, like fruitcake, and frosted sugar cookies. What's a festival without those?"

Carol grabbed a tablet from one of the booths, and people lined up around her.

"If everyone can have the baked goods here by one o'clock Christmas Eve, we'll be in good shape," Allie said.

Carol chimed in. "If it's easier to drop them off at Chris Kringle Kitchen, we will store them for you and deliver them here."

"Thanks, Mom."

Michelle walked over to Allie. "I don't know why I thought I could do this without you. You've saved the day."

"That's not true. You'd have come up with the same idea." She hugged her. "Quit worrying. We have a plan in place now and it will be fine."

"You're the best."

"Don't thank me yet." She turned to Zoe and Ryan. "Are you ready to get back to my house and start baking?"

"Sure!" Zoe bounced with delight.

"We're out of here," Allie said to Michelle.

In the truck, Allie knew she was low on baking supplies since she'd been planning to be out of town for the holidays. "I'm going to have to stop at the store for a few things. I thought we'd do frosted sugar cookies. What do you think?"

"Yes," Zoe said with a fist pump. "Do you have cookie cutters?"

"Of course I do!"

"Why doesn't that surprise me," Ryan said. "And probably in a labeled box."

"Hmm. Don't judge me."

"Oh, I'm not judging. I'm impressed."

"Well, thank you." She straightened behind the wheel. When they got to the grocery store, she left the truck running. "I'll be just a minute. I know exactly what we need. Does anyone have any special requests?"

"Nope."

She ran across the parking lot and in record time came out carrying three plastic shopping bags. She piled them in Zoe's lap. "Ready?"

"I'm *so* ready to bake, and taste test, Christmas cookies." Zoe peeked in the top of the bags.

Allie drove them to her house, backed into her driveway, and led the way up the steps of her front porch.

Zoe went inside first. "I love your house, Allie. And all the decorations are so pretty."

"Thank you."

Ryan started unloading the grocery bags. "Did you forget the cookie mix?"

"No, silly. Sugar cookies are easy to make from scratch."

"Uh-oh." He pursed his lips, making a face causing Zoe to giggle.

"Dad's not that good of a cook." Zoe put her hand on his back. "It's okay, Dad. You try hard."

Their easy relationship warmed Allie's heart. "Well, there you go." Allie was glad Zoe was getting the chance to do some baking. It had always been Allie's favorite thing to do over the holidays. "And we'll help you, Ryan."

Allie gathered aprons for everyone.

"Zoe, why don't you get all the cookie cutters out? They are in a clear box on the second shelf from the bottom in the pantry. Ryan, I'm going to start the dough. Can you preheat the oven to 375 degrees?"

"On it." He set the oven.

"The cookie sheets are above the refrigerator. There's a stool in the pantry."

Ryan laughed. "I don't think I'll need the stool."

"Oh. Yeah. Showoff." She let Zoe crack the eggs and measure out the flour and sugar, and then Allie worked in the rest of the ingredients and piled the ball of dough into a corner of the big bowl.

"Can we play Christmas music?" Zoe asked.

"Sure. There's a stereo over on that shelf."

Allie tossed flour onto the kitchen counter and then rolled dough out onto it. "Ryan, you can roll out the dough." She handed him a rolling pin. "Super easy. Long even strokes, and you want to keep it at about a quarter of an inch thick."

Zoe rushed over with cookie cutters in hand.

They started an assembly line of sugar cookies. Allie making the dough. Ryan rolling it out, and getting pretty darn good at it, and Zoe punching out the shapes with the cookie cutters and placing them on the cookie sheets. They made lots of shapes. Candy canes, Christmas trees, stars, and wreaths.

When Zoe got ready to use the gingerbread shape, Ryan called her out. "Wait a second. You can't make a sugar cookie gingerbread."

The girls ganged up on him. "Says who?"

He tossed his hands in the air. "What was I thinking?"

Eight to ten minutes at a time they switched out baking sheets, carefully moving the hot cookies to the cooling racks.

"Are any of these cool enough to start decorating yet?" Zoe asked.

She loved being able to help Zoe. She'd always thought she'd have a little girl of her own, but a husband and a family just hadn't happened for her yet. "Why don't you try one? For quality assurance. You can test for taste and coolness."

"Awesome." Zoe picked out a star, biting one point off at a time. "These are so good. They don't even need frosting." She held her cookie up to her dad, and he took a bite.

He nodded. "These are great."

"Glad you like them." She turned back to Zoe. "Want to try to decorate a couple?"

Zoe brushed off the flour from the front of her apron and washed her hands again. She took a spatula and spread a thin layer of homemade cream cheese icing on a star, then dropped gold and blue sugar sprinkles on it.

"That looks good," Ryan said.

"Thank you. I'm pretty good at this," she said. "You try it, Dad."

He picked a candy cane cookie, striping it with red and white frosting.

"Good job, Dad."

They frosted and decorated a dozen pretty quickly.

Zoe was eating as much icing as she was getting on the cookies. Ryan nudged Allie, and they shared a quiet laugh behind Zoe's back. She thought she was being so sneaky. At least Zoe washed her hands every time she snuck a taste...if you could even call that sneaking.

Allie handed another bowl of dough to Ryan. He lifted the flour canister and dipped in the measuring cup. "Hey, what happened to all the flour?" He peered over Zoe's shoulder as she squeezed green icing on a small star-shaped cookie.

Zoe set the icing aside. "It's all over you!" She swatted the flour off the front of his red apron.

Ryan laughed and swatted at the dust. "I guess it is."

Allie carried a tray of big star cookies frosted and dusted with gold glitter sprinkles. She set them on the bar. "We're almost out of butter, too." She reached for her keys on the counter below. "You know what? Take my keys." She placed them in Ryan's hand. This felt so natural. She hated to think it would all be over soon.

"Go on down to my parents' restaurant. My mom and dad will have all the extra supplies you need."

He paused. "Zoe, you good with hanging here with Allie for a little while?"

She didn't even hesitate. "Yeah!" She raised her hand in a wave. "Bye, Dad."

Allie was delighted by her reaction. It was fun to have a kid to do these things with at Christmas. She and Spencer had never talked seriously about children, but she couldn't imagine her life without them. Her parents had given her such a wonderful childhood. It seemed only right to pass that along.

"I'll take that as a yes." Ryan got up and took off his apron, hanging it on the back of his chair. "Have fun."

"In the meantime," Allie said, "why don't I teach you how to decorate Christmas stockings?"

"Sure!"

"Come on." Allie slapped the cookie crumbs from her hands and led the way to the kitchen table. She spread wrapping paper across the table to protect it, then went out to the garage and came back in carrying two boxes labeled *Christmas Crafts*. "Look at this."

Zoe got up on her knees in the chair. "You had all this stuff?"

"I love Christmas," Allie admitted. "Can you have too many stockings?"

"I don't think so!" Zoe took the red stocking with the white fur at the top from Allie and set it in front of her.

Zoe is like a mini-me. "My sentiments exactly." Allie put a stocking down in front of herself. "Sometimes I make them for my patients."

"Dogs?"

"And cats. Horses. Cows."

"Like Snowflake!"

"Yes! Exactly."

"I'll make mine, and you can make one for Snowflake." Zoe started sifting through the different designs. "She'll like that."

Allie spread out appliques, and fabric glue. "All we have to do is pick out a theme and figure out where we want to stick the shapes. Then glue them down. Easy-peasy."

"And fun," Zoe said. "It's like we're elves in Santa's workshop."

"You're right. I told you this would be easy and fun."

"It is." Zoe seemed to choose her words carefully. "Be sure to tell Dad. Okay?"

"Why?"

"He doesn't like me to be sad," she said. "He worries about that a *lot* since Mom died. I just like to let him know that I'm okay."

Allie's heart bruised. For the loss, and Zoe's bravery. "But you know it's okay to be sad sometimes too, right?"

"Yeah." She took a breath. "And I am…sometimes. And so is Dad." She pulled her lips into a tight line.

"Well, I think that's normal," Allie said. "But also sometimes you're happy. Right? Like when you think about your mom. Thinking about all the things you two would do at Christmas time?"

Zoe brightened. "Yeah! My favorite was on road trips. We'd play this game where you have to come up with a thing for each letter of the alphabet. Me and Dad play it now."

"I love that," she said. "Wait. What would you do for the letter Z?"

Zoe lifted the stocking she'd been working on with the bright gold letters Z, O, and E across the top. "Zoe!" She held the stocking in the air, showing off the nutcracker. "What do you think?"

"I love it!" Allie picked up a reindeer shape with a candy cane stuck to it. "Look. Who knew reindeer liked candy canes?" She held it up to an empty spot on Zoe's stocking.

"Let's glue him on."

The doorbell rang. "Oops. That's probably your dad." She made a dash for the door. Christmas, cooking, crafts, and Ryan and Zoe were the perfect cast in her fantasy family holiday.

"I'll glue this on while you get that," Zoe said.

Allie zipped through the living room to the front door and swung open the door.

But it wasn't Ryan. Instead, Spencer stood there with arms opened wide, and all her family dreams came tumbling down in a heap.

"Spencer?" She watched a local taxi pull away from her house.

"Surprise."

She couldn't register what was happening. *You were just in DC when we talked. And the road is closed.* "How did you get here?"

"Well," he said with an air of arrogance. "Remember how I told you I have that partner who was going to let us use his helicopter?"

"You took a helicopter here?"

"Yep!" He pointed behind him with a smirk. "Landed just outside of town. Took a cab here." She shook her head in disbelief. "Come on. That's really something, isn't it?"

"Yeah. That's definitely…something."

"Look. I don't totally understand this whole 'one last Christmas in Evergreen' thing, but I couldn't bear the thought of not spending it with you. So…here I am."

"Yes." She stood there not knowing exactly what she was feeling. She should be happy that he'd come all the way to Evergreen in a snowstorm to see her, but she felt almost annoyed. "Oh, I guess. You should come in. Come in."

Chapter Seventeen

Ryan parked in front of the Chris Kringle Kitchen, almost feeling like part of the community himself, and yet he hadn't even heard of Evergreen two days ago. This was the most welcoming place he'd ever been. "Hi, Carol," he called out as he walked in the diner.

"I thought you all were baking cookies with Allie tonight."

"Oh, we are. We just ran out of some things. She said you'd be able to stock us back up."

Carol grinned widely. "Homemade sugar cookies?"

"You guessed it."

"Her specialty. Yes. I know exactly what you'll need." Carol lifted a finger in the air and rushed to the kitchen, leaving Ryan to take in the homey details of the restaurant. Casual family dining at its best. The Early-American-style hutches were filled with dishes. A collection of teapots added to the experience with a punch of color. There were lots of Christmas decorations, too, and rightly so with the name Chris

Kringle Kitchen, but that snow globe near the cash register seemed to drag his attention back to it over and over. If he didn't think Carol would be right back, he'd be tempted to make a wish on that snow globe himself. One that he and Zoe would both feel this happy forever.

A few minutes later Carol walked out of the kitchen with a big box. "Here you go."

"Thank you." The box was filled with milk, flour, butter, sugar, butter, eggs, and even more that he couldn't see in the bottom.

"This should last longer than you all will," Carol teased. "It's hard work baking cookies."

"I have a feeling cleaning up is going to be harder than the baking, but we're having fun with it."

She laid her hand on his shoulder. "I'm so glad."

He walked out of the Chris Kringle Kitchen with the box of ingredients. "Thanks, Carol."

"You got it?" she asked as she held the door for him.

"I do. Thanks so much," he said.

She went back inside, but before Ryan reached the truck, the Santa look-alike ambled up and asked, "Making cookies for Santa?"

"It's for the festival."

The man stepped closer. "It's nice you're doing that."

"It's the least we could do," Ryan said. "Everyone has been so nice to us. Especially Allie."

Santa nodded knowingly.

"I just wish there was something I could do to return the favor."

A twinkle lit in the old man's eyes. "Well, a little birdie told me that she doesn't have a Christmas tree."

He's right. "No… she doesn't. Thank you…uh…I didn't catch your name."

"I'm Nick." His red cheeks swelled as he smiled. "Merry Christmas," he said, stretching the words out in that good old-fashioned way. He toddled off, and Ryan stood there. *If I didn't know better, I'd believe he really is St. Nick.* The rosy cheeks, twinkle in the eye, the chipper walk, and that 'Merry Christmas.' It was a perfect imitation.

Ryan opened the passenger door of Allie's truck and slid the box onto the floorboards, then walked around and got in.

A Christmas tree for Allie. It was perfect. She'd love that. He wasn't sure if he could get back to the tree lot that they'd gone to together to get the one for Barbara, but the town wasn't that big. He'd figure it out.

The truck chugged down the street. At the stop sign in front of the gazebo, he turned left, in the opposite direction of Allie's house. Two streets up there was a Christmas tree lot on the corner. Not the same one, but it would do fine.

Candy cane striped PVC pipes held up a brown sign with alternating red and green letters that read *Christmas Trees For Sale.* Colorful pennant flags hung around the perimeter, making it a little more circus than Christmas, but he was sure he could find a tree for her here.

The two smallest trees they had were potted, not cut. That seemed a little over-ambitious, since she'd be moving to DC. Planting a tree here in her Evergreen front yard was one thing. Expecting her to haul it to DC to stick it on a condo patio? Probably not the best present.

Plus, those trees weren't the least bit scraggly.

Knowing her reputation for the underdog tree, he continued to look for something that needed a little TLC. There was one that had a bare spot in the back. He couldn't bring himself to buy that one though.

There were a few others that would never earn the Miss Best Christmas Tree trophy even in a lineup of three, but he didn't want to take her something less than perfect after the kindness she'd shared with them.

He took another stroll through the lot. It was slim pickings on the eve before Christmas Eve. *Why is this so hard?*

He knew exactly why it was so hard.

Because it mattered.

Forget what I know about her liking the underdog trees. Think about how she makes me…us…feel.

He turned around and as soon as he did he was facing the prettiest tree he'd ever seen. He lifted the tag. A Fraser fir. He leaned in closer. The aroma was strong. It smelled like Christmas.

Unlike most of the trees on this lot, this one had

a blue-green color to it, and the way the tips of the branches cupped up made it look eager to be decorated.

"This is the one," Ryan said. "It's perfect." *Like her.* He lifted the tree right up off its stake so no one else could claim it, and carried it to the cashier. "Sir?"

The young man at the cash box jumped from his chair. "Oh, wow. I guess you picked one already! We'd have gotten that for you."

"That's okay. It's not that heavy." Although he'd gotten some sap on his jacket. "I'm in a hurry."

Ryan paid the man and carried the tree to the truck himself. He couldn't wait for Allie to see the tree. It had been a more-than-perfect day, and this was going to be the perfect ending to it.

He could barely contain himself as he revved up the truck and retraced his route back to the Chris Kringle Kitchen, and then took the road he knew back to Allie's house. His cheeks almost hurt from smiling. This was the best surprise, and he knew Zoe was going to be absolutely delighted that he'd bought a tree, too.

Feeling somewhat like a superhero who'd just saved the world, he honked the horn as he backed into her driveway. His heart sped up in anticipation of seeing their faces when they saw the tree.

Chapter Eighteen

Allie still couldn't believe that Spencer had flown in a helicopter, in a storm, to visit her for Christmas, unannounced. She stepped aside so Spencer could come in. He walked into the kitchen then stopped.

She'd been so focused on the pretty cookies that she hadn't even really paid much attention to the whopping mess they'd made. But clearly by the look on Spencer's face…he'd noticed. The mess did seem to spill all the way to the dining room table where she and Zoe were now working on the stocking projects.

She shoved a cup of cocoa into his hand. "Here. I made some cocoa."

"Thank you." Spencer pulled off his coat, revealing his designer button-down shirt and conservative blue suit. He took a sip of the cocoa, glanced at Zoe, who was busy working on her stocking at the table, then turned back to Allie. "Who's this?"

Allie tugged on her old blue sweater, feeling

underdressed in her own house. "Oh, this is Zoe. Zoe, this is Spencer."

"Hey, Zoe," Spencer said. "How do you know Allie?"

Zoe grinned that winning smile of hers. "Me and my Dad met Allie in town and then at the airport and we all got stranded, so we made snowflakes and then we came here and a cow gave birth—I named her Snowflake—and there was caroling, we built a snowman, and now we're making Christmas cookies for the festival and stockings just because it's fun!" She held her stocking up for him to see. "Allie's making one for Snowflake."

Spencer looked at Allie like he didn't understand a single word that had just blown past him. "Snowflake? Someone else I should know?"

"No. Snowflake is a calf. They were with me when Henry called." Allie wrinkled her nose. "I was just going to say 'it's a long story,' but I think what Zoe said pretty much sums it up."

"You're making a Christmas stocking for a cow?" Spencer didn't seem impressed.

"Technically it's a calf," Zoe said. "Allie does things for a lot of her patients. She's a good animal doctor."

He shook his head like he couldn't be bothered to figure it all out.

Allie kept an eye on Zoe as she worked on her stocking. Ryan would be here any minute.

Spencer took a sip of the cocoa, then leaned against

the kitchen counter. "So, you just brought this guy and his kid back here?"

"Yeah. Kind of." She sensed his hesitation. "It seemed like the best option..." *Is he mad?* "...at the time." She didn't want to apologize for inviting them back. Being with them was so much fun. And what was wrong with helping others, anyway?

"Right." After a two-beat pause, he said, "Listen. Did this have anything to do with you wanting to stay in Evergreen for Christmas?"

"No!" She waved her hand in front of her. "No, that was all me."

"Okay."

Only she wasn't sure how convinced he was. But it was the weather. She had no control over that.

A double-honk broke up the awkward silence, and Zoe ran past them to the front door. "Dad's back!"

Spencer let out an exaggerated sigh as Zoe and Allie raced for the door. He placed his mug on the counter. Allie opened the door and stepped out onto the porch, Zoe stepping outside right next to her.

Ryan stood at the back of her truck with a box full of baking supplies. "Hey." He let go of the box with one hand and lifted the tip of the tree with the other. "What do you think?"

"You got a Christmas tree!" Zoe exclaimed. "I can't believe you got a Christmas tree."

He jogged up the sidewalk with the box. "Yeah, well...it's for—" He stopped in front of the steps, just as Spencer stepped up behind Allie.

"Oh, this is Spencer." Allie's heart caught in her throat. "Spencer, this is Ryan."

Ryan paled. "Spencer? Washington D.C. Spencer?"

"That's right." Her smile was forced. He'd brought her a tree? Her heart pounded in the fastest version of "Deck the Halls" known to mankind.

"Yeah." Zoe gave a very impressive nod. "He flew here in a helicopter."

"Really? Can we borrow it?" Ryan grinned, but he looked more like he'd like to disappear right now.

It was incredibly awkward, and Allie was pretty sure she could feel her kneecaps shaking…and not from the cold.

"Uh, no, they just dropped me off." Spencer sounded annoyed. "So who's the tree for?"

"It's for Barbara," Ryan blurted out. "At the inn."

"But…we just got her a Christmas tree," Zoe said.

Spencer raised a brow.

"Right. Well…" Ryan rambled. "We got her a tree for the…for the living room, and this tree is for the lobby. The lobby Christmas tree. Because at Christmas time, you can never have too many Christmas trees. Am I right?" He looked at Allie, hoping for the best.

She forced a smile, nodding in agreement. "You're right."

"So listen," Ryan said. "We should go. The road might be open tomorrow, and you know if that's the case, we can get ready to get on out of here."

"Right. Escape from Evergreen," Spencer said.

Ryan shifted the box in his arms. "Exactly."

Allie jumped in. "Why don't you take my truck with the tree in it to Barbara's house, and then we can walk there to see if she's got a room for Spencer in a little while."

Ryan walked up the steps and handed the box of supplies to Spencer. "Thank you. Yes. That's a good idea. Spencer. Nice meeting you."

Allie reached in and grabbed Zoe's coat and handed it to her.

"You, too," Spencer said. "Bye Zoe."

Zoe waved. "Bye." She pulled on her coat as she ran down the steps to catch up with her dad, who was already heading for the truck.

"Let's go, kiddo. Let's get on out of here." Ryan hotfooted it toward the truck.

Allie and Spencer stood on the porch until they pulled out of the driveway.

"You okay to walk?" she asked him.

"Well, it's no helicopter, but sure," he said, followed by a cocky chortle.

What kind of response is that? She forced a laugh. "I'll get my coat."

Spencer followed her inside, carrying the box to the kitchen.

The night was brisk but the wind had settled down so it wasn't too bad. Allie had wanted to share Evergreen with Spencer for years, but now that he was here it wasn't anything like what she'd dreamed of. They walked down Main Street. She saw the town and the cheery holiday lights and displays everywhere with fresh eyes, but he didn't even react. He kept talking about DC.

Trying to break the ice, she said, "I still can't believe you took a helicopter to get here."

"Pretty cool, huh?" He looked pretty pleased with himself.

"Doesn't it seem a little...extravagant?"

"It only seems like that because you're not used to it yet."

"Nah, you know me." She glanced across the street at her vet office. "I have simple tastes. I'm an Evergreen girl."

"And now you're going to be a DC girl."

"Yeah." *But I'll still be me. That's just geography.*

"Come on, Allie, aren't you just a little excited about starting your new life? Aren't you happy to finally be getting out of this little town?"

"I love this place." She couldn't imagine ever feeling this kind of joy in the hustle and bustle of DC. "I know it might not seem like much to you, but this is my hometown."

He didn't seem even the teensiest impressed, and that bothered her.

"I mean look around," she said. "This is what Christmas is supposed to be like." The resounding joy in Zoe's voice when she'd come out of the diner that first day they'd met played back in her memory. That response was what she'd expected from Spencer, too.

"I get it. I know you have a soft spot for this place. That's why I came all the way here to be with you."

"I know." She leaned in. "And I appreciate that, but aren't we supposed to be taking things slow?"

An impish grin crossed his face. "That's why I had to see you."

Her heart caught in her throat.

"I don't need to take things slow." He looked into her eyes. "I know what I want." He paused. "The question is, do you?"

She grappled for air. She wasn't ready for this.

They'd said they'd take it slow. Test the waters. And after the last couple of days, she wasn't sure what she wanted.

She glanced around at the town she loved so much.

No, she wasn't sure at all what she wanted at this moment. But she didn't know how to tell him that either.

Across town, two high school teachers maneuvered the twelve-foot Frosty the Snowman into place in front of Henry's barn. Like Frosty, the festival was coming to life and excitement filled the air, but it was coming down to the wire, and Michelle was stressing out over it.

Volunteers scurried around, and the choir was practicing. Michelle had decided to stay a while longer tonight to knock out a few of the things on her to-do list before calling it a night, even though she'd been at it since early this morning.

She lifted strands of lights from a box and plugged

them in to test them. They lit, but were one tangled mess. She growled at the sight of it. *Why can't people put things up nicely at the end of the season?*

Hannah saw her tussling with the lights. "Hey, Michelle."

Michelle spun around to see Hannah standing there dressed in a red Christmas sweater covered in Scotty dogs with rickrack leashes. On top of that, she wore that chipper smile. "Hannah? Why aren't you at home making fruitcake? You're in charge of fruitcake," Michelle snapped.

"I finished," she said with a shrug.

"Well, then make something else!"

"Half the town is cooking. We're going to have enough food for, like, five festivals." Hannah giggled.

Forever the optimist; that was the last thing Michelle needed right now with all that had gone wrong so far. "There is no such thing as *enough* when it comes to a Christmas feast." Her hands shook.

"Oh." The smile slid from Hannah's face.

Michelle pulled and tugged on the strand of lights in a holy terror.

"Okay, Michelle." Hannah placed her hands on Michelle's arms and guided her to a chair nearby. "Do you want to have a seat over here?"

Michelle groaned.

Hannah placed a caring hand on Michelle's shoulder. "I think you need to relax."

"I can't. I have too much to do." Michelle shook the lights with each word.

"And there's plenty of time to get it all done. It's going to be fine."

"It can't be fine. It has to be incredible." She fought back tears.

"It will be. You're doing an amazing job."

Then why did she feel like everything was falling apart around her? "It's just...Allie made everything look so easy."

"Allie had a lot of help. She didn't try to do it all by herself."

"Yeah." Michelle leaned her head on Hannah's shoulder. "Okay." She stifled a laugh. "Maybe I should go make a wish on the Christmas snow globe."

Hannah sat quiet for a half beat. "Well, you wouldn't be the only one."

Michelle twisted in surprise. "You made a wish? What did you wish for?" It was hard for Michelle to imagine Happy Hannah needing to wish for anything. She always seemed on top of the world.

"Well..." Hannah fidgeted. "I don't know if you know this, but I just love Christmas."

Michelle feigned surprise, and then stared at Hannah's sweater. "No! I didn't know."

They laughed, and Michelle tugged on one of the sparkly gold leashes on Hannah's sweater. The girl had to have a different sweater, or maybe two, for every day of December.

"I... This is going to sound silly...but I wished to find someone special. Someone who loves Christmas as much as I do." She looked so hopeful.

Michelle paused. If anyone deserved that kind of happiness, it was Hannah. "That's not silly. It's sweet."

"Really?"

"Mm-hmm." Michelle really hoped that old snow globe came through for Hannah.

"I just figured, what could it hurt? It's Christmas. A time when magical things happen." Her eyes glistened with hope.

Michelle loved the hopeful and optimistic attitude of Hannah. *She's right. It is the season for wonder and special gifts.* "How late is the diner open?" She grabbed Hannah's hand. "Come on."

They got in Michelle's car and drove over to the diner. They had some business with a snow globe to take care of.

Chapter Nineteen

Ryan and Zoe drove back to the inn in silence. He couldn't believe Spencer had shown up. It had been awkward enough, but if Spencer had waited one more moment before stepping out, Ryan would have been in the middle of announcing he'd bought the Christmas tree for Allie. That would have been much worse.

How was it that he couldn't get out of the town, but this Spencer guy whisked right in unannounced? In a helicopter?

"I thought of a helicopter first," Ryan mumbled.

"What?" Zoe perked up.

"Nothing." He hadn't realized he'd said it out loud.

Zoe looked at him. "You know, you should have really gotten the tree for Allie's house."

No kidding. If only… But he didn't have a right to be upset. He knew that, but it still didn't make it any easier. "Yeah. That would have been nice."

"I really like her."

He sucked in a breath. "So do I." And even more

than he'd realized. Spencer showing up was like losing electricity in the middle of your favorite movie. A sucker punch at the end of an otherwise perfect day. Before the man had shown up, Ryan would've said that he hadn't felt this happy in a long time, and Zoe too. She'd worn a smile of true happiness since they'd been in Evergreen. He loved seeing his little girl's eyes light up like that.

He pulled the truck up to the inn and took the tree out of the back.

"Can I go tell Barbara?"

"Sure."

Zoe ran to the porch and opened the door. "Barbara! Come see," she called in from the doorway.

"What's going on, Zoe?"

Ryan schlepped the tree into the lobby.

"Another tree?" She cocked her head.

He wasn't sure if she was happy or not. "Yes! We thought it would be nice for your next guests."

"Thank you." She pulled her lips together, as if coming up with a plan. "I'll make it a winter tree, and keep it up for the whole month of January."

"That sounds perfect," Zoe said. "Can I help decorate it?"

"Of course," Barbara said. "Where's Allie?"

"Her friend Spencer showed up," Zoe offered. "He flew in on a helicopter to see her. Is that cool, or what? They are going to come over in a little while."

"Oh?" Barbara looked confused and when she turned toward him and caught his gaze, Ryan turned his attention to the other room. He couldn't answer

175

Barbara's questions any more than he could soothe his own. "Well, isn't that nice. It's wonderful to spend time with friends and family over the holiday."

"Want me to get the leftover decorations from the garage?"

"It's getting late," Barbara said. "We can work on it tomorrow."

Zoe's smile faded.

Ryan hated seeing her disappointed. "Zoe, we'll probably be leaving in the morning."

She slouched. "I'm going to miss this place. I love staying here, Barbara." She ran over and gave her a hug.

"I'm so glad you were my very first guests. I'll never ever forget this visit, or the beautiful trees."

"You'd better head to bed, kiddo." He watched his daughter climb the stairs.

"Do you have another tree stand?" he asked Barbara.

"I do. Right here in the closet. Let me grab it." She opened the heavy door in the hallway and walked out with it. "Ta-da."

"Great."

She moved a coat rack and umbrella stand to make room in the entry hall, then set the tree stand in the corner. "That'll look lovely. Thank you."

"You're so welcome." He knew he was really just making more work for her though. He'd pictured tonight going much differently. He lifted the tree and lined it up in the stand, then dropped it down on the spike. "Is it straight?"

She stepped back and checked both sides. "Perfectly."

He tightened the bolts.

Barbara carried a pitcher of water over to fill the tree. "Thank you so much, Ryan. I'm really going to miss you two. I hope you'll come back and stay with me again."

"We've really enjoyed our stay." He couldn't make any promises he'd ever be back. "Oh, I'm going to leave Allie's truck keys here in the foyer. She said she'll pick them up later."

"That's fine." Barbara finished filling the tree stand, then put the pitcher down. "Ryan, is everything okay?"

"Yeah. Sure. I'm just going to go to bed." He gave a little stretch, pretending to be tired. "Hopefully, we'll be on our way to Florida in the morning. I'd better get some rest."

"Good night."

He went upstairs. When he peeked in on Zoe, she was already fast asleep. He packed his suitcase and set his alarm, then lay across the bed, trying not to think about today. Or Evergreen.

Allie was ready to go back home and crawl in bed. She didn't even care if the kitchen mess got cleaned up tonight, and that wasn't like her.

She and Spencer walked down Main Street. "Let's get you settled in over at Barbara's." She walked, keeping conversation to a minimum, leading the way over to Barbara's Country Inn and hoping like heck that Barbara could put Spencer up in a room for the night.

He kept talking about them flying back to DC tomorrow, which was the last thing on her mind tonight, so she mostly listened and smiled. This wasn't her idea of taking it slowly.

"Here we are." Allie turned up the walkway.

"Charming," he said, but she got the feeling he was placating her.

"It's awesome, and Barbara is great. You'll love her." She hurried to the door. "Come along." She knocked on the front door of the inn and walked inside. "Barbara?"

"In here," Barbara called from the living room. "Hi. Who do you have here?"

"Barbara, this is Spencer. He's from DC. Any chance you can put up one more guest tonight?" *Please say yes.*

"Of course. My pleasure. This is the best pre-opening occupancy rate I could ask for." She turned to Spencer. "Now please keep in mind that the inn isn't officially open just yet. You'll have to bear with me, but I'm happy to have you stay. I promise when you come back in the future, I'll have every perk in place." She gestured them inside. "You two just missed Ryan and Zoe. They called it an early night."

"I see you got the tree," Spencer's accusatory tone annoyed Allie.

Barbara steepled her hands under her chin. "Wasn't that so thoughtful? He is the nicest man."

Spencer seemed to be waiting for Allie's reaction. Instead of responding to Barbara's comment, she said, "I'm going to leave you to get settled in, Spencer. I'm beat. It's been a long day. I'll see you in the morning, and hopefully the road will be opened back up."

Spencer cocked his head. "So soon? You don't want to sit and chat? Catch up a little?"

"I'm really tired. All that Christmas festival stuff and the baking. We baked dozens and dozens of cookies for the festival. I still have a few to finish decorating before I go to sleep."

"Oh."

"You have been busy," Barbara said. "I made something to help out too."

Spencer looked confused.

Allie felt the need to explain. "With the road shut down, the people who were supposed to make the food got stuck out of town. Everyone had to pitch in to keep things going."

"I see."

"Yeah. Crazy day," Allie said. "I'm just going to—"

"Your keys are on the table there," Barbara said.

"Yes. Thank you. I'm going to get my truck. And go home. And go to bed."

Spencer hugged her. "And if all goes according to plan, flights will be running again in the morning. We'll make this a wonderful Christmas yet."

But she was already having a wonderful Christmas.

He turned to kiss her and got her cheek. Something didn't feel right. He was aggravating her with his rush to get back to DC when she'd already been very upfront with her plans to stay put.

She knew he liked getting his way. He was pretty used to it, but this was the first time he'd steamrolled her to get it. She didn't like it.

She slipped out from under his arm and headed to the door. "Sleep tight."

She had no intention of leaving Evergreen now even if the flights were running. Had he really come all the way here just to get her to go there?

Chapter Twenty

The next morning when Ryan woke up, things were quiet at Barbara's Country Inn. He was up and dressed early as usual, but mostly because he was eager to get out of town.

Zoe was still asleep so he finished packing his things, and then repacked hers except for what she'd be wearing today. It could end up another long travel day, so until he knew the flight was a go there was no reason to wake Zoe up.

He went downstairs to grab a cup of coffee and see if he could find out anything about the roads and the airport.

As he turned the corner from the stairs, he stopped short. Sitting there at the royal-blue-and-white tile farmhouse table was Spencer, messing with his phone.

Allie had said she was going to see if Barbara had a room for Spencer, but he'd thought she was just being polite, assuming Spencer would stay at her house last night. He did get an ounce of satisfaction out of knowing the man hadn't.

Ryan stepped into Barbara's big country kitchen, trying to seem aloof. "Hey. How's it going?"

Spencer put down his phone. "Hey. I was just checking flights to DC here." Spencer put his hand over his mug, motioning to the coffee Barbara had prepared for them. "Coffee?"

"You're not taking the helicopter back?"

"No." Spencer laughed. "That's a favor we can only use one time."

"Oh? We?" Ryan grabbed the coffee carafe from the table and poured a cup for himself. "I thought Allie said she was staying here for Christmas."

"Well, she was, but we talked last night and I'm hoping she might change her mind."

"Oh...well, that's...that's good." He sipped his coffee.

"Yeah." Spencer seemed to be struggling for the right words. "I think once we get back to DC and she gets settled in her new job, it's going to be smooth sailing." But the words were much more confident than his body language. "So..."

The sound of the front door opening and footsteps coming toward the kitchen halted their conversation. Allie walked in, slowing to a stop and making the slightest gasp of surprise when she laid eyes on both Spencer and Ryan—together.

"There she is." Spencer bounded from his chair and came around the table to greet her with a kiss.

"Hi." Allie turned her head away just as Spencer came in for the kiss, leaving him once again with her cheek.

"Hi." Spencer wrapped his arm possessively around her waist.

"Hey," she said to Ryan.

"Hey."

Her smile was tight. "Hi," she said again to no one in particular.

Ryan felt responsible for the awkward situation they were all in this morning. He'd gotten carried away. Maybe he should go make a wish on that snow globe to turn back the last twenty-four hours. Or at least the part where he'd shown up with the tree.

Allie held a steady forced grin, and for a moment no one said another word.

Zoe stepped into the room and stared at them. "Why is everyone just standing around?"

"Uhh. We should go," Allie said. "To the diner. Ezra was going to stop by and give us an update of the roads. About the roads. On the roads." She let out a breath. "Whatever." She turned and headed to the door.

Zoe shrugged.

"Great?" Spencer said.

Ryan rolled with it. "Yeah." He followed Zoe, who was right behind Allie.

"Okay." Spencer grabbed his coat from the back of the chair and headed outside to catch up with Ryan, Allie, and Zoe for the short walk to the diner.

When Allie, Spencer, Ryan, and Zoe reached the Chris Kringle Kitchen, Carol was already pouring cups of coffee to a room full of more than twenty locals. Most of the festival volunteers, along with Nick, looked like they'd been there for a while, if the empty breakfast plates were a good indicator. Everyone was eager to know if the road in and out of Evergreen would be opened today or not.

Ezra showed up a few minutes later. He stood in front of them with an air of authority he hadn't earned yet. Standing at the back of the diner, he called everyone to attention. "Listen up everybody. I have an update on the road situation."

Everyone stood and lined up to get the latest news.

Ryan stood behind Zoe, his hands on her shoulders. "Is it open?" he asked hopefully.

"It's not," Ezra announced matter-of-factly.

There was a collective groan, and Michelle let out a loud moan of disappointment. Allie felt bad for her. She'd worked so hard on the festival, and Allie knew from experience that the festival wouldn't be the same if it were only for Evergreen.

"But!" Ezra raised a brow and lifted a hand in the air. "It will be by tomorrow night, so we can have the Christmas eve festival the next day as planned." Ezra was so pleased with his little act there that he started applauding for himself.

There was a cheer this time. People shook hands and clapped, and Allie saw Michelle step over to the snow globe and say, "Thank You."

Who could blame her for wishing on the snow globe for things to work out? It did seem as if everything that could go wrong had gone wrong. But her friend had risen to the occasion.

"You're going to love it," Allie was saying to Spencer as Carol grabbed her arm and tugged her away. "I'll be right back."

Carol dragged her to the side. "Spencer flew in on a helicopter?"

Word sure had traveled fast. "Oh, Mom, don't start," she stage-whispered.

"What happened to it not being a big deal? This seems pretty big."

"It's not." But it was. How could she play something like that off? Who had access to a helicopter? In a snowstorm? She was still having trouble wrapping her head around it herself. "It was a small helicopter." That was a lame rebuttal and she knew it. She had no idea if it was a small helicopter, and in any case, what did it matter?

Her mother's expression made it clear that the explanation hadn't helped. "What about Ryan?"

"What about him?" She was not up to dealing with all of this today.

"Allison Louise, I can tell there's something happening between you two."

"It's not. It's nothing. No, there's not. Nothing's happening and it's no big deal." She smiled through clenched teeth, but her hands were fisted in aggravation. If only Spencer hadn't shown up. Although part of her was glad to have seen this side of him now. She escaped from her mom's prying questions and headed over to where he and Ryan were standing.

Spencer put his arm around her and rubbed her neck.

Allie forced herself to act happy as she spoke to Ryan. "So that's good news. You'll be able to head to Florida after all."

"Yes, that is great. Zoe, isn't that great news?"

"Yeah. It's great." Zoe slipped away from her dad. Allie watched her walk over to counter. She didn't look very happy. "I'm counting on you!" she said, wagging her finger at the snow globe.

That globe was getting a lot of action today. What had Zoe wished for? The girl folded her arms on the counter and propped her chin on them, staring at the snow globe as if she were daring it to let her down.

Who was Allie to judge? She'd made her own wish on it the other day, too.

"I guess we know all we needed to know. Are we ready to head back?" Allie asked.

Spencer nodded, and Ryan and Zoe fell in step behind them. Allie opened the door, and they all stepped out onto the sidewalk.

"This is terrific." Spencer stopped out front of the diner. "If the road opens by tomorrow night, we can still make it to Washington D.C. for Christmas."

Allie sucked in a breath.

"I mean," Spencer continued, "if that's what we decide that's what we want to do, of course."

She glanced over at Ryan. "Right," Allie said. "We just have to decide…"

"Right," Spencer said.

Allie smiled at Ryan and Zoe. She'd miss them. "Well, since we'll all be here at least a little while longer. What do you want to do?"

Nick walked out of the diner. "Good afternoon." He tipped his face to the sky as if enjoying the soft falling snow. "Beautiful weather for ice skating." Then with a quick nod he was off, his red scarf trailing over his shoulder.

"Can we go ice skating?" Zoe asked with delight.

"Oh! That sounds fun," Allie said. "There's a gorgeous ice skating rink in town. Should we all go?" She turned to Spencer, whose phone was vibrating in his pocket.

"Yes!" Zoe said.

"Yeah, that sounds great," Ryan agreed.

"I'd love to," Spencer said, holding his phone. "But I've actually got a conference call and it could take a couple of hours."

"Oh." Allie was disappointed. It had been a long time since she'd skated. It would be so much fun with Zoe too, but she should probably stay back with Spencer. "Okay."

Spencer raised his hands. "But you guys go ahead, and I'll catch up with you later."

"Wait. Really?" Allie's mood buoyed. "Are you sure?"

"Yeah." He rubbed his hand along her back.

"Okay." She turned her attention to Zoe and Ryan. "Well, now we just need to find y'all some skates!"

"Yes," Zoe said with a fist pump.

"Okay, well, we're going to head to the rink," she said to Spencer. "We'll take the back way so we go by my house so I can get my skates and to see if I have a pair in my garage that will fit Zoe. You can walk with us, or just go straight to the inn."

"Okay." He put his hand at the small of her back protectively. Allie tensed at the gesture. "I'll see you when you get back."

"Okay. Great." Allie stepped over next to Ryan and Zoe.

Spencer gave them a nod. "Have fun."

She and Ryan and Zoe started walking toward her house. Was it her imagination, or did something in Ryan's expression change as they walked down the street? He seemed happier. More relaxed.

Zoe, on the other hand, was amped up to be going skating.

Chapter Twenty-One

Ryan was thankful Spencer had a conference call and couldn't join them. That guy just didn't seem like a lot of fun. He let Allie lead the way to her house, but when they got there, he lifted the garage door for her.

Allie and Zoe went inside to start the ice skate hunt. It shouldn't have surprised him that she made a beeline right to her skates. She brushed the dust off them and set them aside.

"Been a while since these have been used," she said with a laugh. She glanced over at Zoe. "Are you going to be warm enough?"

"Sure."

"Wait a second." She darted into the house and came back with a cream-colored infinity scarf and two pairs of gloves. She draped the scarf around Allie's neck. "That's better. My mom made that for me."

"It's so pretty. Thanks."

"And gloves." Allie put her gloves on, too. "We're ready for ice skating now."

"Yes!"

"How about you, Ryan?"

"No girly scarf for me, thank you."

"Ha ha." She moved a couple of cans of tennis balls over and pulled out a pair of pink ice skates for Zoe. "These were mine when I was little. I wonder if they might fit you?"

"I hope so." She tried them on. "They are a little bit big, but I think they would work."

"Let me see." Allie pressed her thumb down on the end of the skates. "I think one more pair of socks and if we lace them up nice and tight, you'll be all set." She moved things back into place. "Now we just have to find skates for your dad. I bet my dad has an old pair that will work. We'll walk down to Mom and Dad's on the way. Dad never throws anything away."

"Sounds like a plan," Ryan said.

Her parents' house was less than a block away. "It must be nice to be so close to family," he said.

"It is." She punched in the code on the panel at the garage door, and it lifted.

This garage was just as organized as hers. *Like father, like daughter.* What habits of his would Zoe would carry on? Hopefully not his messy handwriting. Or working too much.

Allie led the way to the back right corner. On the wall there was an assortment of sporting equipment: everything from badminton to water skis. On a wooden board there were at least ten pair of ice skates from when he coached the teen hockey team. "Jackpot," Allie yelled.

Zoe ran over to check them out. "They look brand new."

"My dad is fanatical about taking care of things. They're probably better than new." She turned back to the rack. "What size do you wear, Ryan?"

"Eleven and a half. A twelve would work."

"No problem. Here are two pairs." She raised them in the air. "You choose."

Ryan picked out the pair that fit him best, then carried them to the door. "This is great, Allie. Thanks."

"I think we have everything we need. It's going to be fun!" They stepped outside, and Allie pressed the button to close the garage bay door behind them. They walked down her driveway to the sidewalk. "This way," she said, leading the way.

Zoe skipped ahead of them, swinging her arms and pretending to do ice skating tricks on the sidewalk.

Ryan shifted the pair of skates in his arms. "Where did the day go?" It was already starting to get dark.

"I know. I hate that it gets dark so early this time of year." Then she brightened. "Then again, we get to enjoy the Christmas lights that much longer."

"That's true."

Zoe stopped at the corner. "Which way?"

Allie pointed to the left.

"Wait up," he said.

Zoe twirled until he and Allie caught up with her. "We're almost there," Allie said.

A couple of blocks ahead, lights adorned huge cedar trees. A white cross-board fence outlined the skating rink filled with holiday skaters.

"Now that's cool." Ryan wondered what his life with Sarah would've been like had they chosen that small-route all those years ago, rather than starting his practice in the city. He'd been young and eager. Maybe being older now, he could appreciate it more. His priorities had definitely changed over the years.

The closer they got to the skating rink, the louder the laughter and chatter filled the air like a song. The energy was contagious.

They took off running, all three of them, and found an empty bench to change into their skates. Right behind them, the Snack Shack served hot cocoa, bags of freshly popped popcorn for a quarter, and a selection of cookies. On every decorative lamppost around the arena, fat red ribbons streamed from wreaths made of mittens in every color imaginable. Holiday music instrumentals filled the air, and the skaters filled in the words.

"Ready?" Allie stood. Zoe took her hand.

He pushed up from the bench with a wobble. "I think so."

The three of them joined hands and stepped out onto the ice. Other skaters whizzed by. They took it slowly the first lap around.

Finally, they were all getting the rhythm of the strides and sailing across the ice with ease.

Ryan held his arms out for balance. "This is a lot of fun. I haven't skated in forever."

"Years," Allie said. "For me it's been years."

"Has it?"

"Yeah. So, a lot more recently than you."

But they were all skating at a comfortable pace now. Like riding a bicycle. He tugged on Zoe's hand and whipped her and Allie around in a circle. They cheered as they picked up speed.

"Whoa! I'm going to take a break." Allie slid to a stop at a nearby bench.

"Okay." Ryan dropped to the seat next to her. "Have fun, Zoe."

Zoe pushed off with her right skate and sailed across the ice with her arms gracefully slicing the air. "I feel like I'm flying!"

Allie placed her gloved hands on her knees and managed, out of breath, "Does Zoe ever get tired?"

"No," he said, huffing. "She would stay out here all night if you'd let her."

"How could there be that much energy in such a tiny little body?"

"Medically speaking, it's impossible. Nobody knows."

They lapsed into silence, enjoying the moment as Zoe skated back and forth in front of them. She was quite graceful and was picking up speed and turning nicely, too.

Ryan's cheeks hurt from smiling. He loved spending time with Allie, and that smile on Zoe's face was better than a lifetime of cruises from Florida. He noticed that Allie seemed contemplative. "Is everything okay?"

"What?" She almost seemed startled. "Oh, yeah. Great."

Selfishly he wanted her to be enjoying their time together. Before he could stop himself, he said, "Because if you want to go spend time with Spencer, I totally get it."

"No. This is fun, and he's working anyway. It's fine."

"He seems like a good guy."

She paused. "He is."

He wished he hadn't brought Spencer up.

"You know, I always..." She cleared her throat. "I always thought that we were in the same place even though we lived far apart. We always saw things the same way. Wanted the same things. But..." She shifted her gaze toward the trees. "Now that we're going to be living in the same place, I don't know that it's that true anymore."

"What do you want?"

Allie looked at him, their gaze holding the question.

Realizing how that must have come across, he tried to correct. It wasn't any of his business. He made a jokey smile. "I mean, like, for Christmas. Like, what's your wish list for Santa?"

Relieved for the reprieve, she took a quick second to consider. "Ohh. A pony."

"Probably more reliable than your...truck." He positioned his hands like they were on a steering wheel and cringed, knowing she had a soft spot for that old truck.

"Hey, don't knock my truck. That's my grandpa's truck. I love that truck."

"I'm your mechanic, so I do, too. Seriously, it's got character." *And it had brought us together.*

"That was my grandpa. A real character," she said, beaming.

"You were close?"

"So close. I miss him so much. He always had wise sayings for any situation. Oh, and he loved to draw. He did these beautiful, snowy scenes of people taking sleigh rides and sledding and getting their Christmas trees. It felt like home."

He understood. "It felt like Evergreen."

"Yeah. I guess that's what I really want for Christmas. My grandpa used to do these great drawings on postcards. I always wondered why he didn't do, like, a big picture or something, but anyway, he did these great drawings of the town. He'd done them ever since he was a kid. He told whole stories with just the pictures he'd drawn."

"That's neat."

"Yeah. It is. I never got any of that talent. But when I'd look at those drawings, I would feel so connected to this place. I'd get this…this feeling of exuberance. That's what I want. I want that feeling I got from my grandpa's drawings."

"More than a pony?" he teased.

Allie nodded. "More than a pony." She seemed

to be off in her thoughts somewhere. "So to answer your question about what I want." She paused, and then took a leap of faith. "I think what I want. Is to feel… I want to always feel the way that I do here in Evergreen." Her smile was bright.

"The feeling of home."

"That's it." She took in a breath. "Yes. Exactly. So, how about you? What do you want?"

He could get used to this. Allie sitting at his side. Talking on a cold night as they plan something fun together.

Zoe's laughter filled the air. They watched her skate, free as a bird, arms wide and enjoying the night with a huge grin on her face.

"That." Ryan glanced over at Zoe. "That's all I need." Love filled his heart. He was so blessed to have Zoe. When he turned back, Allie was looking at him with a kindness, a softness about her that overwhelmed him. He laughed nervously.

Zoe skated by and yelled, "Come on, guys!"

"I'm going to check to see if she has a battery pack or something."

They laughed, and then her phone rang.

"I've got a phone call." She took her phone out of her pocket. "Oh. It's Hannah." She answered the phone as Ryan bent over to tie his skate. "Hey. Whoa, what's going on? Yeah, he's right here."

Ryan sat up and leaned in closer, sensing something was wrong.

"Okay. All right. We'll be right there as soon as we can. Okay, bye." She hung up the phone.

"Is everything okay?" he asked.

"I'm so sorry to do this to you," Allie said, "but we need a doctor."

Ryan called for Zoe. "Let's go."

Zoe swished by and spun in front of Ryan. "I'm not ready to go. Can we just do two more laps?"

"Sorry, kiddo. There's an emergency. They need a doctor. We need to hurry."

"I'll call my dad to pick us up and give us a ride, while you help Zoe. We need to get out to Henry's barn."

They quickly shed their skates and changed back into their shoes.

"He's going to meet us on the corner," she said. They picked up their skates and jogged to the corner. Joe pulled up just as they got there, and they piled inside his SUV. "Thanks, Dad." Allie slammed the door shut. "Everyone inside and buckled up?"

"Yep."

Joe took off. "What happened?"

"I'm not sure," Allie said. "Hannah was frantic. She said Michelle was lightheaded and disoriented." They rode in silence. Finally, Joe took the turn down Henry's lane and pulled up in front of the open door of the barn.

Ryan jumped out of the car and ran inside. Hannah was standing next to Michelle. "What happened?"

Hannah wore a pretty red sweater with snowflake

trim and a very concerned look. She placed her hand on Michelle's shoulder. "I don't know. We were working on the festival and then she started to get all woozy and… Is she going to be okay?"

"No, I'm not okay," Michelle said, frantic, flailing a length of pine roping with poinsettias and pinecones wired to it around like a scepter.

Zoe froze in her steps just behind her dad.

"Honey," he said to Zoe. "Give us a moment, okay?"

"Okay." She turned and walked over to where there was a box of ornaments sitting next to a tree and started to place them on the branches.

Ryan turned his attention back to Michelle. Her hands shook, and beads of sweat were forming on her forehead.

"We don't have enough garland. The barn is…" She gulped air. "And outside… And in two days. There's not enough time and there was supposed to be…"

"Okay, Michelle." Ryan stooped down in front of her to get her attention. "Michelle, I need you to breathe, okay?"

She drew her hand to her heart, tears springing from her face as she shouted, "I don't have time to breathe!"

"Michelle," he said calmly, "do you remember 'The Twelve Days of Christmas?'"

Allie glanced up to the ceiling, as though she thought he was crazy. Michelle narrowed her eyes.

He began to sing. "On the twelfth day of Christmas,

my true love gave to me..." He smiled gently. "What was it?"

Michelle choked out the words. "Uh...drummers. Twelve drummers drumming? Right?"

"Yes," he cheered. "That's right. What's next?"

"Pipers piping?" Her eyes darted around as if there'd be clues in the room. "Eleven?"

"Right. Keep going."

"I don't know ten," she struggled. "I don't know it." She squeezed her eyes shut.

Allie chimed in. "Lords..."

Michelle perked up. "Ten lords a leaping. Right! And then it was nine ladies dancing, uh...eight maids a milking..." Her words came slower.

Ryan gave her a nod, encouraging her to continue.

She took in a breath. "Swans, geese, five golden rings, four calling birds, three French hens, two turtle doves..." She let out a sigh, then sang, "And a partridge in a pear tree."

Hannah and Allie laughed with relief.

"Good," he said. "How are you feeling?"

"Better." Michelle eyed him. "What did you do?"

"You were having a panic attack. Counting is one of the things that can help alleviate it. I just thought we'd stick to a Christmas theme." He stood up, relieved it wasn't anything more serious.

Allie's reassured gaze caught his attention. "Are you okay, Michelle?"

"I am. I just... I was really crazy to think I could do this as well as you have for so long," Michelle said.

"Oh, don't say that." Allie lifted her arms. "This is amazing."

Ryan stepped closer. "Let me tell you something…I have never seen a group of people more dedicated to anything in my life. The way you have pulled everyone together and turned this place into… I mean, come on, look at this."

They all took a moment to slow down and take in what had been accomplished.

The barn had been transformed into something festive and fabulous. Every single beam was wrapped in fresh garland. Every piece hand-tied and lit. An impromptu stage for the choir and performances had been set up at the far end and somehow, Michelle had rigged up a plush red curtain as the backdrop, giving the place a warm, welcoming feel.

The empty slate of Henry's brand-new barn had been transformed into a magical place, ready for the townsfolk to gather and celebrate. No easy task.

Ryan felt suddenly a part of something. Part of this great group of people in this special little town. "This is what Christmas is about."

"That's true," Allie said wistfully.

"The festival is going to be great," Ryan said, "and it's all because of you, Michelle."

She lowered her head. "Thanks, Doc." Hannah hugged her.

The children's choir started singing another traditional Christmas tune.

Allie noticed Zoe right in the middle of the group.

She grabbed Ryan's arm and pointed her out to him. They watched for a moment, smiling and enjoying seeing Zoe so happy.

Allie motioned toward the door. The tents and games were still being worked on outside when they came out of the barn.

"That was impressive in there," Allie said.

"You birthed a cow," he said. "I think that wins the battle of impressive things that happened in barns."

"Thank you."

"You're welcome." He wanted to reach for her hand. Allie was incredible on all fronts. Ryan held her gaze for a moment and then glanced over his shoulder. "I should..."

She nodded, and he turned to go back inside.

Allie was about to stop him when her phone rang. She looked at the caller ID. She glanced back at him, and then answered the phone. "Hi, Spencer."

Ryan's mood dipped. He turned and went back into the barn to check on Michelle. He had no right to feel what he was feeling right now anyway.

Chapter Twenty-Two

The next morning Spencer had meetings, so Allie went to the diner to get breakfast. The place was packed as usual. She scanned the room for a seat with someone she knew. Nick sat in what had become his regular table in the back. She spotted Zoe and Ryan at a middle table eating breakfast. Allie maneuvered through the tables to where they were seated. "Mind if I join you two for breakfast this morning?"

"Sure," Zoe said.

"Thanks." Allie grabbed a mug of coffee from the back counter and then came back and sat down at their table. She and Ryan sipped coffee while Zoe indulged on hot chocolate with marshmallows. She was pretty sure Mom had been behind prescribing hot chocolate for breakfast. It wasn't even in the regular mug they used, but in one of the ones Mom loved so much: extra big, so there was lots of room for marshmallows on top.

Ryan was quiet, leaving Allie missing the playfulness they'd been enjoying together.

"Hello, you two." Carol approached the table. "Homemade Christmas cookies." She placed the plate of assorted cookies in the center of the table between them.

"Thank you very much," he said. "These look delicious."

Carol stepped behind Allie and hugged her. "Allie's a very good baker too, by the way."

How embarrassing. Mom is making those cookies sound like a dowry. She couldn't have been more obvious that she liked Ryan a lot. Not that Allie could blame her. He did make a pretty powerful first impression.

"I know. We've been baking cookies for the festival." He glanced across the table at Allie with a nod.

Not only had they baked a ton of cookies, but it had been one of the best nights she'd had in a long time.

"That's right. You have. That must have been so much fun," Carol said.

Joe called out from behind the counter. "Hey everybody, Ezra just called." He waved his phone in the air. "And great news."

Everyone in the diner gave him their full attention. You could've heard a fork fall.

"The road will be cleared tonight," Joe announced.

The silence was replaced with cheering.

Allie spotted Zoe over near the front counter by the register. She was staring into the snow globe, her brows knitted together. Then she shook her finger at it. "I thought we had a deal."

Nick walked over to her. "What's wrong, Zoe?"

She turned, slack-jawed as if she'd been caught. "I made a wish and I thought it was coming true, but now I'm not sure." Her displeasure was clear.

"Oh?" Nick's own brow furrowed. "Well, was it something your heart truly wanted?"

"Yes! All of me wanted it. Even my toes!" She stuck out her boot and gave her foot a wiggle to prove it.

Allie almost spit coffee through her nose. That little girl was absolutely adorable.

Nick let out a hearty laugh. "In that case, I don't think you have anything to worry about."

"Are you sure?" Her face was etched with worry. A single wrinkle formed across her forehead just like the one Allie had seen on Ryan when he'd been worried at the airport.

Allie had a feeling she knew what Zoe's wish was. Like her, she loved Christmas in Evergreen. They were two peas in a pod. Allie hoped Zoe's wish came true.

"I'm sure," Nick said. "You just have to be patient. Wishes are like Christmas cookies…it sometimes takes awhile for them to be fully baked."

Ryan noticed Allie watching Zoe. "I'd better get her. We're going to need help eating all of these cookies."

"For sure." Allie picked up a cookie and dunked it into her coffee.

"Zoe?" Ryan stepped behind her and squeezed her shoulders gently.

"Hi," Nick said.

"Hi," Ryan said politely. "Kiddo, your hot cocoa is getting cold." He turned her shoulders toward their table. She took off toward Allie with a smile, and he began to follow.

Nick stopped him. "What about you, Ryan? Have you changed your mind about making a Christmas wish?"

He shook his head. "No. I don't really believe in that sort of thing."

"You know, people get busy…and they forget about the magic of the holidays," Nick said gently. "But all they have to do is stop for a moment and open their eyes. Because that magic…it's all around us." Nick patted Ryan on the shoulder as he passed by on his way out of the diner.

Had he believed in the magic of the holidays before his wife passed away? That had to have been such an awful thing to go through.

Ryan stood there for a moment, thoughtful. Nick had a point. It was like those times in church when the sermon seemed like it had been written just for him.

Allie handed Zoe a gingerbread cookie. "For you. Everything okay? You were in deep thought over there."

"Yep. Everything's okay. I'm just going to be patient." Zoe bit the head right off of the gingerbread man.

That poor gingerbread was taking a beating over that wish. Allie glanced back over toward Ryan. He was holding the snow globe. Maybe Nick's comment had resonated with him too.

Her heart swirled. Had he made a wish? She looked over at Zoe, who was dancing her headless gingerbread man across the table in a chorus of "Jingle Bell Rock."

When Ryan came back, he wore a broad smile.

Allie was dying to ask him about his wish but didn't want to let on that she'd been watching him, or that she'd overheard the conversation with Nick.

Zoe sipped her cocoa.

"When you finish your cookie, are you ready to go back to the inn?" he asked Zoe.

"Sure."

A heavy, dark ache settled in Allie's chest. She was going to miss them. They got up and headed for the door. Ryan stopped and pulled out his wallet.

Carol wagged a finger at them from the register. "No, sir. You will not pay today. That was my treat." She gave him a wink.

"Thank you. Everything was delicious."

"Thank you!" Carol zipped around the counter. "You forgot your cookies. I'll box them up. Zoe, come with me."

Allie and Ryan stepped outside to the sidewalk. Without even the plan to do so, they both stopped and took in how pretty the shops looked today.

In that moment, she felt such a connection. A sense of place. An alliance to this town. To Ryan. To that sweet little girl, Zoe.

She pulled her keys from her pocket. "You can just take the truck and leave the keys at Barbara's. I'll get them later."

"Thanks." He shoved his hands in his pockets, never taking his eyes off her. "This really is a special place."

"Yes. It is." Allie didn't want this to end. This… whatever it was…was good. She braved a smile, but her insides were anything but cheerful. The fake smile hung like a pit in her stomach. "So, you're all set?"

"We are." He nodded slowly. "Off to Florida."

"That's what you wanted, right?"

"Yea." His expression seemed sad.

She wished they'd stay.

"And you. You're off to DC."

That seemed like a million years ago. "Yeah. That's the plan." There was no reason to tell him otherwise. He was just passing through. The stuff with Spencer was hers to work through.

"Looks like we both got what we wanted."

She wanted to say no. That this wasn't what she wanted. To urge them to stay. She wanted to say it so badly. Instead, what came out of her mouth was, "Looks like it."

But looks could be deceiving. Their eyes held, until he dropped his gaze to his shoes.

"Ryan…"

He turned to her, and hope filled Allie's heart…but then she couldn't do it. She couldn't put her feelings into words. She hesitated so long that she finally just said, "Merry Christmas."

She wished instead that they were laughing about what they were going to do next instead of saying goodbye. Christmas cruise cows, snow gorillas, self-ies with Frosty, flour messes while baking cookies, anything!

"Merry Christmas." His voice was gentle.

Allie smiled through her disappointment. So that was all it was meant to be.

"Allie?"

She sucked in a breath, hoping he'd say what she was thinking.

"I. I wanted to— Um." Ryan stammered.

"Hey! Allie!" Zoe shouted as she came out of the diner. "Will you promise to send me pictures of the festival?" She counted off on her fingers. "I want to see the stockings, the choir, and the tree." She pointed her finger at Allie. "Don't forget the tree!"

"Well, I won't. I promise. It's the only tree I have this year!" She glanced at Ryan, and then hugged Zoe. "Merry Christmas, Zoe."

"Merry Christmas, Allie."

Still holding Zoe to her chest, she rested her cheek to Zoe's soft hair. Would she ever be so lucky to have a little girl like Zoe of her own? Her heart warmed, feeling more whole for having had this time with them. She didn't want to let them go.

She straightened, letting go of Zoe. Her warm heart pinched as if the edges were being singed. It hurt to know she'd never see them again.

She turned to face Ryan. His blue eyes seemed sad. Or maybe that was just what she wanted to see. "Merry Christmas, Ryan."

"Merry Christmas, Allie."

Allie already missed them. There was a heavy void in her chest, but there was nothing more to say. She forced herself to walk away, crossing the street back to the diner.

Ryan watched Allie walk away. Her soft brown hair swished against the back of her coat, and his good mood seemed to be leaving with her. When he'd watched Allie with Zoe at the table, dancing their gingerbread men across the table, he'd had a moment of euphoria. He wasn't ready to lose that.

This could be the last time he'd ever see her.

His breath caught. He hadn't realized it until this moment, but she'd reopened his heart. This short accidental meeting in a town he'd never heard of...it had changed him.

"Dad?"

He pulled himself from the thought and turned back. "Yeah?"

With all the innocence of a child, Zoe lifted her chin and looked him in the eye. "Where's Santa going to leave all of Allie's presents if she doesn't even have a tree?"

His little girl's eyes filled with worry broke his heart. She was such a sweet child, with a generous heart.

And then it struck him.

Why let Zoe worry? He could fix this.

"Jump in the truck, Zoe." His heart raced. "Buckle up."

He started the truck and took off. Zoe stared out the window at the shops. "I'm going to miss this place."

"Me too." But they were going to make one more stop before they left this town for good. It was the least he could do. For Allie, for Zoe, and for himself.

"Dad? You just passed the inn." Zoe looked at him like he was cuckoo.

"I know."

"Where are you going?"

"We're going on a mission."

She grinned. "Am I going to like this?"

"You are going to love it." One more turn, and he was back at the Christmas tree lot.

"We're getting Allie a tree?"

"It was your idea," he teased. "You ready to decorate one more tree?"

"You bet!" She jumped out of the truck. "Can I pick it out?"

"Any one you want."

He didn't even care if the tree was perfect or not. He needed to get a message to Allie, and this was how he intended to deliver it.

Zoe picked out a tree, and interestingly enough it was a beautiful Fraser fir like the one he'd picked out for Allie originally, only as he got closer he noticed something extra special about this one.

"Zoe. Look."

She tiptoed to see where he was pointing. "It's a little bird's nest."

"It sure is."

"Dad, that has to be lucky."

"That's exactly what I was thinking." He lifted the nest from the branches. "Here, why don't you hold on to this until we get to Allie's? We can put it back then."

She held it delicately in her hands as he talked to the lot manager.

"And I was wondering, do you have a tree topper? And any ornaments?"

"I've got this star tree topper. The only ornaments I have left are these clear plastic ones."

"I'll take them all."

The lot manager started stacking the boxes together. "No problem, man. I'll put them in the truck for you."

"That'd be great," Ryan said.

The guy wrote up the ticket and handed it to the cashier. "He'll get you settled up while we get everything loaded."

"Oh, I'll need ten boxes of those white lights too. And one of the extension cords." Ryan handed over his credit card. "Am I forgetting anything?"

"Got a tree stand?"

She probably had one, but he didn't want to be rifling through her things. "You'd better toss that in too."

Zoe danced alongside him. "This is so awesome."

"I hope we can get there and get it set up without her seeing us," he said.

"We'll be super fast." Zoe did a little jig. "Like Santa's elves."

"You're all set." The cashier handed him his credit card back. "Merry Christmas."

"Merry Christmas to you." Ryan dug a twenty-dollar bill out of his pocket as a tip and handed it to him. "Thanks for all of your help. Merry Christmas." He and Zoe ran to the truck. "You ready for this?"

"Mission Tree Lighting. Top Secret." She took Allie's sunglasses off the dash and put them on. "I accept this mission."

Ryan laughed out loud. "I see that."

They drove over to Allie's. "How do we know she's not here?" Zoe asked.

"Good question." He thought for a second. "Tell you what. You run up to the door and ring the bell. If she answers, tell her that you wanted to say goodbye. If she doesn't answer…wave me in."

"You got it, Dad." She clamored out of the truck, her jacket hood bouncing on her back as she ran up the stairs to ring the bell.

He held his breath, hoping the surprise would work out. A moment later, Zoe was waving him in with big wide arm gestures. He ripped the keys from the ignition and carried all the boxes to the door. The second key he tried from her key chain worked. "We're in," he said. He laid the boxes down. "You move these on into the living room. I'll be right in with the tree."

"Got it." By the time he got inside with the tree, Zoe had laid all the supplies on the dining room table for easy access. "Where are we going to put the tree, Dad?"

"I've got a plan." And when he said those words, it made him think of Allie. She always had a plan. When she got that impish grin and her eyes lit up followed by "I've got an idea," he never knew what to expect, except that it was going to be good.

Ryan moved the boxes she'd stacked up in the living room to the sun porch, then slid the chairs over, opening up the corner. Where the lighted ficus tree had stood, there was now a tall Christmas tree. They got the tree in the stand in the corner.

"Dad. This tree is perfect."

"It is, isn't it?" He turned and grabbed a velvety soft throw off the couch on the other side of the room and draped it under the tree as a makeshift tree skirt. "Zoe, you start putting the hooks on all of those clear ornaments, then stack the boxes right here by the tree as you get that done. I'm going to get these lights on in a hurry."

"I'm on it, Dad."

He was about halfway through putting the lights up when Zoe said, "Too bad they didn't have any colored ornaments."

He finished stringing the lights, then got down on his knees and plugged in the tree.

"Light test!" They both stood in the middle of the room and squinted.

Zoe said, "Yes!"

"It looks good."

"Good? No way, Dad. It looks awesome."

"Let's get these ornaments on." They double-teamed placing the ornaments on the tree. Ryan hung all the high ones, and Zoe covered the bottom half. "That's all of them."

He carried the empty boxes out to the sun porch and tucked them in the corner out of the way. He didn't want to leave a mess.

"Dad, I never would have believed it, but those clear ornaments with the lights make the prettiest Christmas tree I've ever seen."

He wrapped his arm around Zoe's shoulder. "I think so too, kiddo."

"We'd better skedaddle before she catches us."

"I've got one last thing to do. Go jump in the truck. I'm right behind you."

Chapter Twenty-Three

*L*ight snow fell as Allie made her way down Main Street. She should've been home hours ago, but she'd made a hollow excuse to help out around the diner. Not because she was being helpful, but because she simply wasn't ready to be home alone yet tonight. She also needed time to figure out what she was going to say to Spencer. His surprise trip to Evergreen had been eye-opening.

She walked along the block of shops she knew so well. The decorations and merry lights usually made her happy, but tonight she felt lonely in their midst.

The town gazebo sat empty tonight. So many happy things took place here in the town square, but tonight it seemed unusually quiet. Probably because everyone was across town at Henry's place getting ready for the grand finale. The Festival.

Every year since she'd come back from college and set up her clinic, she'd run that festival. From start to finish, she'd plan, negotiate, purchase, craft, and coordinate the event into a night to remember.

Suddenly, she realized not working on the festival this year had left her with an unexpected gap. She missed it. It was part of her.

She reflected on the previous years. There were always last-minute problems, and a scramble to get things right, but in the end the festival always delivered. Walking here in the quiet snow, it occurred to her that the festival's success had never been based on how good a job she'd done. In the end, it was really all about the people of Evergreen. The fellowship they shared as they rejoiced over the holiday, making memories they'd carry with them not only all year long, but for every Christmas going forward.

Someone was sitting on the park bench in front of the gazebo. As she got closer, she saw that it was Nick.

"Good evening," he said.

She continued walking in his direction. "Good evening."

"Are you ready for the Christmas festival tomorrow?"

"Yes. I am. Are you?"

"I'm definitely ready for Christmas." Nick hopped up from the bench with a bright smile. "It's a time when wishes come true."

"I always thought that."

Nick's brows knit together. "But you don't anymore?"

"No, I'll always believe in Christmas wishes. But... what if you don't know what to wish for?"

He paused. "Is this about leaving Evergreen?"

"I—"

"…or Spencer?"

Allie's jaw dropped. "How did you know that?"

"It's amazing what you learn while sitting at a table in the town diner."

"Right. Of course." That made perfect sense. She relaxed a little. "Well…I guess it's kind of about both."

"So what did you wish for on the snow globe?"

"I wished that everyone I love would have a Merry Christmas even though we can't be together."

"And yet here you are, in Evergreen, with all the people you love." He lifted his chin.

"But I'm supposed to be in Washington D.C.," she explained.

"The further away you are from where you started, the closer you get to where you belong."

Allie recited the last part along with him.

He couldn't know that from just sitting in the diner. Grandpa used to always say that. It was practically the whole reason she'd dreamed of leaving Evergreen for so long. An emotional tidal wave lifted inside her, making her eyes tear.

He spoke slow and directly to her heart. "Sometimes you end right back where you started, because that's the place you're supposed to be."

His smile and message warmed her, but she was overcome.

She swallowed back tears. Her grandpa had been the wisest man she'd known. He was the whole reason she was so driven to go places, to see the world…to find where she belonged even though she loved her life here in Evergreen. It had never occurred to her that this was where she belonged.

And Zoe had said the same thing. Wise beyond her years.

Was it true? Was Evergreen where she was supposed to be all along?

She choked out a gasp, trying to hold back the flow of tears.

"Oh, my dear." Nick put his arm around her to comfort her. "There, there."

She held him tight until she could pull herself together. She stepped back, running shaky fingers underneath her eye to sweep away the tears.

"Good night," he said and walked away.

"Good night." *That was the strangest thing. Did that really just happen?*

Things suddenly seemed so clear. The sadness she'd just been carrying had lifted.

She stood there for a long moment, and then walked at a fast clip through the streets of Evergreen toward the inn. Everything was dark. Rather than disturb Barbara, she used the hide-a-key to get her truck. She'd get the key from Barbara another day.

Thankful the truck started on the first try, she drove home, thinking about the cyclone of emotions over the last few days. And especially tonight.

She parked in front of her house. "Grandpa, I still miss you." She patted the steering wheel, and then opened the door and walked up the sidewalk. As she started to take the stairs, she almost let out a yelp. She hadn't expected Spencer to be standing on her front porch. "Hey. Spencer? What are you doing here?"

"I wanted to stop by." He stood there in jeans and a leather jacket. "I think if we leave first thing in the morning, we can still get to the airport and make it to the firm's Christmas Eve party."

Allie stepped by him and unlocked her front door. "Right. The *swanky* one?"

"Yeah, the swanky one."

She swept passed him, but he followed along.

He seemed to notice her lack of enthusiasm. "Allie, what's wrong? Don't you want to go to DC?"

"I'm so sorry, Spencer." She couldn't do this anymore. She didn't know what her future held, but she was pretty clear on what wasn't in it. She at least knew now that Evergreen was where she belonged. She tried to be gentle. "I think I want to stay here."

He shook his head. "For Christmas, or..." His eyes narrowed.

"For Christmas and...I don't know," she said. Trying to not let him down, she added, "But why don't you stay here for Christmas? I love this place and I love these people and I want you to understand why."

"Allie, I love Washington D.C. And I love my job and the people I work with are really great. I mean, that's where I belong."

She nodded, tears brimming, and took his hands in hers. "Spencer, I don't think it was just the distance that was getting in our way."

"Allie, don't do this. Okay?" Shaking his head, he whispered, "Please?"

"You do belong in Washington D.C. And I don't. I belong here."

"But what about your new job?"

"I love my job here." He'd been great to tell her about that job lead, and it had sounded exciting, but it wasn't what she wanted. She loved her small-town patients. "I get to take care of tiny little puppies and I get to birth calves. That's incredible!" The enthusiasm as she said those words lifted her spirits. "And I have a family and friends and Christmas in a place that I love."

"I think you're just nervous about making such a big change." He spoke softly as if trying to calm her down, but that wasn't it at all.

"Well, you see, I think that's the thing. I thought I was ready for this big change…and I am…but I think I thought I had to leave Evergreen to find it. I kept telling myself that I needed more when everything I needed was right here all along."

Spencer squeezed her hands. "What can I do to convince you that I'm right about this?"

There was nothing he could do or say. She'd never been so sure of something in her life. Tears filled her eyes. He cared about her, but DC wasn't where she belonged, and Spencer didn't love the things that made her happiest. "I think you'd be trying to convince yourself." She kissed his cheek, then patted his arm, hoping he understood. "Merry Christmas, Spencer."

"Merry Christmas, Allie."

He let go of her hands and walked out.

It had been the hardest conversation to have, but she was thankful she hadn't had to think or plan it. It had just come out. The way it was supposed to.

Her life was here. She was where she belonged, and that made her happy. She walked into the kitchen and flicked the light switch, but instead of the ficus that she'd strung lights on in the corner by her favorite reading chair, that corner of the room glowed, illuminated by Christmas lights on a festive tree in the corner.

Allie gasped. The only color on the entire tree: a single bright red envelope with her name on it in big block print letters.

She walked over to the tree and pulled the envelope from the center branches where it was propped.

Her hands shook as she opened it and pulled out the Christmas card inside.

The card had a simple pine wreath with a red ribbon at the bottom a lot like the one on her front door. Inside the handwritten note read,

Allie,

Zoe was worried that Santa might not have a place to put your presents if you didn't have a tree. We hope you get everything you want for Christmas. Even the pony. Thank you for everything.

Ryan and Zoe

Tears pooled, spilling to her cheeks as she looked at the tree and hugged the card to her chest.

She squinched her eyes together, and there wasn't one single spot on that tree that wasn't lit. *Good job, Ryan and Zoe.*

The only present she wanted was on its way to Florida.

She changed into her favorite pajamas, the ones with the black pants with little red Christmas bows on them and red long-sleeved top. Back in the living room and picked that card back up off the coffee table, and sat in the chair by the tree, pulling the blue-and-white blanket over her. She fell asleep by the glow of Christmas lights that night, clinging to the sweetest gift she'd ever received.

Chapter Twenty-Four

A llie woke up with the red envelope still in her hand. It was early, but she was anxious to do a couple of things this morning, even if it was Christmas Eve.

She walked down to her office and tugged the FOR SALE sign from the wall under her placard. That felt good. She tossed it into the nearby trashcan. She wouldn't need that again.

Across the way, Mom and Dad were already busy in the diner. The smell of fresh sausage mingled in the air.

She walked up to the front door of the clinic, unlocked it, and went inside. There was nothing on her books. She'd referred all her customers to Dr. Meyers in Montpelier, but she wasn't worried. Her patients would come back to her. She'd take the down time to reorganize things. Maybe catch up on some bookkeeping.

She sat in her desk chair and spun around. She was home. All that was missing right now was Frank.

She dialed the diner from her office line.

"Allie? Is everything okay? What are you doing at the clinic on Christmas Eve morning?"

"Nothing is wrong, Mom." She took in a deep, steadying breath. Confident in her decision. "Mom, I'm not going anywhere. The doctor is in."

"Oh, Allie? Are you sure? If this is a joke, it's not funny."

"Positive. Why don't you bring Frank back home?"

"I'm on my way. Start the coffee," Carol said.

In less than three minutes, Carol was standing at the reception desk with Frank's goldfish bowl in her arms and tears of joy in her eyes.

"Home sweet home, Frank." Carol put the fish bowl on the desk. "Honey, I'm so happy." Her eyes sparkled, her lips quivering as she smiled.

"Hi, Mom." She hugged her, and then bent down toward the fish. "Welcome back, Frank."

"So? Have you talked to him?"

"Yes. He went back to DC."

"Oh, honey, not Spencer." Carol gave her that look. "Ryan."

"Why would I talk to Ryan?"

"Allie, he bought you a tree!"

"Oh." *It wasn't like it was a ring.*

"He bought you two trees, if you count the one at Barbara's."

"Mom, it's not like that." Well, maybe it could've been. She'd wanted so much for them to stay. Certainly some of the joy of spending time with them had come from the good deed of helping them when they'd been stranded—at least, that was what she'd been telling herself all night.

"I know." She stepped back. "I know." She put her fingers to her lips and pretended to lock them.

Like that could stop her.

"And I'm not saying that what happened with Spencer had anything to do with Ryan. Those are two totally separate things. But Allie, they are both… things. And I just want to make sure you're okay with how *both* of them ended."

Allie considered that for a moment. She wasn't okay with it at all. It was more than just temporary. He'd shown more than kindness in his acts, too.

She grabbed her mom's arm and turned over her wrist to check the time on her watch.

"They might not have left yet," Carol said, encouraging her.

Allie zipped around the desk, only stopping to say, "I love you." Mom had noticed that something special between them, too. She kissed her mom on the cheek, then rushed out the door.

"Hurry," Carol called out with a wave.

She ran out the door, not even bothering to close it, hopped down the stairs, and ran to her truck. She got behind the wheel and put her fingers on the key, only pausing long enough to say, "I know this is the right thing to do. Please start!"

The engine turned right over, and she let out a yip as she pulled away from the curb and headed straight over to Barbara's Country Inn. Her heart raced. Oh gosh, she had no idea what she'd say, but she couldn't wait to find out.

For a split second she worried Spencer might still be at the inn too, but there wasn't much chance of that. He was predictable. He'd have left at the crack of dawn.

Please let that be true this morning. If there was a six o'clock morning flight to DC today, he'd have been on it.

She swung into the driveway and ran to the side kitchen door. With a quick knock, she opened the door. "Hello?"

Barbara was drying dishes when she came in. "Allie! What are you doing here?" She turned, still holding a dishtowel in her hand.

No one else was in the kitchen. "I was hoping to catch Ryan and Zoe before they left."

"Oh, I'm sorry, sweetie." Barbara glanced at her watch. "The cab picked them up about an hour ago. They're probably already at the airport by now."

Her heart caught. She'd missed her chance. They were headed to Florida for the holiday.

Why hadn't she said something when she had the chance? Why had she been too afraid to tell him what she was feeling? "That's too bad. I'd really hoped I'd catch them."

"I have to thank you for the customers, Allie. This has been a great test run for the inn, and I loved every single minute of it."

"I'm so glad. It's beautiful. You and this inn, you're

both a wonderful addition to Evergreen." Barbara had been so kind to open her doors to strangers with so little notice. She truly did fit in here in Evergreen.

"Too bad you're leaving. I think we'd have been great friends," Barbara confided in her.

That touched Allie's heart. "Oh, I'm not leaving after all. Evergreen is where I belong."

"You're kidding? That's great."

"Yes. Yes it is," Allie said with a smile. "And I'm sure you're right. We'll be great friends, and thank you again for putting Ryan and Zoe up. I think you made their Christmas. Too bad they won't be here for the festival." At least she'd be able to send the pictures to Zoe as promised. She hoped their Christmas in Florida would be fun, too.

"Are you ready for the festival tonight?" Barbara asked.

"I am. I need to take all the cookies we baked last night over there though. Do you have anything I need to take over for you?"

Barbara crossed the room to the white breakfront. "I do." She lifted three boxes and handed them to Allie. "Can you take these truffles I made?"

"Truffles?"

"A box of peanut butter truffles and two boxes of whipped chocolate. They are so easy to make."

"You are definitely going to have to teach me." It wouldn't be the same as baking with Ryan and Zoe. Probably not as messy either though.

"Any time," Barbara said. "Thanks for delivering them to the festival for me."

"My pleasure. I'll see you there tonight."

Ryan and Zoe sat in the gate area at Burlington International Airport, waiting for their flight. The terminal was once again busy, and he was having a real déjà vu moment. He had to admit, though, that he was disappointed that when he looked back behind them, Allie wasn't there this time.

"I told you we were leaving too early, Dad."

"Well, with all the cancelled flights and holiday travelers, better safe than sorry."

"I guess."

An announcement came over the intercom. "Ladies and gentlemen in the terminal for flight 993. We have been informed that there is a small mechanical issue on the plane and we will need to delay boarding. I apologize for the inconvenience."

Ryan sighed. Flight 993. That was their flight. He glanced over at Zoe, then folded his arms across his chest and got comfortable. "Boy, that sounds familiar, huh?"

He'd expected disappointment, or maybe an eye roll, but instead she perked right up. "We should go back to Evergreen!"

"Zoe, the flight is delayed, it isn't cancelled."

"So if it gets cancelled, we can go back to Evergreen?" That kid would make a great lawyer. She could negotiate and reason anything. She was quick about it, too.

"No, honey." Evergreen wasn't an option anymore. As wonderful as it had been, now he almost wished they'd never stopped there.

"But don't you miss it already?" Her longing tone was real. She wasn't kidding around. "Don't you miss Allie?"

More than you know. He sighed and wrapped his arm around her. "She isn't mine to miss. Come here." He pulled her close, laying his head against hers.

Zoe was all he needed.

But if that were so, would he be feeling this way right now? Empty, and hurt. Yes. He missed Allie.

Soon she would be starting her new life in Washington, D.C. with the high-powered helicopter-riding Spencer. It was hard for him to picture Allie with that guy. Even harder to picture her in a busy city the size of DC. That was selfishly biased, though, because he had no problem picturing her with him and Zoe anywhere...even DC. He'd love to take her to the Cherry Blossom Festival. And the beautiful covered bridges in Virginia near the scenic byway of Skyline Drive and the Blue Ridge Parkway. It was gorgeous there.

He had a feeling guys like Spencer didn't do things like that, though.

Almost an hour passed, and Zoe was getting fidgety.

"It shouldn't be much longer, honey." Ryan was

getting anxious himself. He could've driven himself and Zoe to Florida and gotten a tan by now if he'd just left when they'd gotten delayed the very first time the other day.

"It's okay, Dad."

"I'm going to go see what's going on. I'll be right back." He got up and walked over to the counter, waiting to talk to someone who might be able to give him a more specific update.

The man in front of him turned to leave.

"Oh, hey. Spencer?"

"Hey. What are you doing here?"

"We're still trying to get to Florida. You?"

"I'm still trying to get to DC. Seems like all the flights are booked though."

Ryan scanned the gate area. "Is Allie here?"

Spencer deflated. "No. She's...staying in Evergreen." He swallowed. "Permanently."

"Oh." A pulse of joy coursed through Ryan, but he held himself in check. "I'm really sorry."

"Thanks. I'm going to go check with the other airlines, see if I have better luck. Merry Christmas." He reached for Ryan's hand.

They shook hands. "You, too."

Ryan let the whole situation sink in for a moment as Spencer walked away. He didn't even bother to ask for an update at the counter; instead, he went back over and sat next to Zoe.

"What's wrong, Dad?"

He was almost stunned. Allie staying in Evergreen

was the last thing he'd expected Spencer to say. But Ryan was glad. Very much so, because he agreed that Allie belonged there. She was the heart of that town. "Nothing." He couldn't contain his smile. "This Christmas…"

"It's been the best!"

"Really? You think so?"

"It felt like Christmas again. Like before Mom…"

Her statement shocked Ryan, but she was right. This Christmas had been easy, and fun, and memorable. He put his arm around her. "It did."

She let her hands drop to her lap. "I just don't understand why the snow globe didn't work."

"What did you wish for?"

"That we could have Christmas in Evergreen."

Ryan's expression fell. How had he not picked up on it?

"But Florida will be great, too," she quickly added. "Did you make a wish?"

"I did," Ryan said. "I wished for a merry Christmas."

"And did it come true?"

"Zoe, as long as I'm with you, it's going to be a very merry Christmas."

"So your wish came true." She looked away. "I wonder why mine didn't?"

She was wistful, and that made him sad.

The gate attendant came over the PA again. "Attention in the gate area, all passengers for flight 993 to Orlando. I'm sorry to tell you that we are having some mechanical difficulties with the airplane and at this point it looks like we're going to have to cancel the flight."

Everyone groaned, except for Ryan and Zoe, who both sat there smiling.

"Maybe your snow globe wish is going to come true," he said.

"Dad? Really?" She bounced up. "Can we go back to Evergreen?"

"I think we should."

Zoe threw her arms in the air and leaped. "Let's go!" She grabbed her bag, and then clasped his hand.

They made haste out of the airport. Ryan steered them through the crowds of travelers into the taxi area. It only took a few minutes to finally get to the front of the line.

"Where to?" The taxi driver lifted the trunk and tossed their bags into the back.

"To Evergreen."

"Little town up route 7?"

"That's the one."

"I've heard of that place. Never been there though."

"It's the best Christmas town ever," Zoe said. "With the best Christmas Festival too." She slapped her hands on her legs. "Dad! I can't believe we get to go to the festival."

"Merry Christmas." The taxi driver reset the meter and pulled away from the curb.

Chapter Twenty-Five

"We're Going to Have a Happy Christmas" blasted through the temporary speakers of Henry Holloway's barn, and the 48th Annual Evergreen Christmas Festival was in full swing. Allie felt at home among the people of Evergreen, and lots of folks had traveled from as far as Montpelier and Burlington to join in the Christmas Eve celebration.

Before stepping into the barn, Allie had taken a quick detour to the barn to check on Snowflake. The barn had been quiet except for the soft neighing of the horses and an occasional moo. When she'd gotten to Buttercup's stall, she'd been standing vigil over her sleeping calf. Snowflake had been snuggled in what was left of the hay bed Zoe had made for her. Allie had stepped into the stall and checked Buttercup's udder. It had been soft and full. A good sign. She hadn't disturbed Snowflake since she was sleeping. Buttercup had leaned her head down toward the baby and made soft maternal sounds. She was a good mother.

Allie walked back outside for some air. She noticed

that sometime during the day they'd found a way to get the banner moved from Town Hall over the entrance of this barn. Michelle had said that the Evergreen Electrical Coop guys were supposed to be coming out with a couple of boom trucks to help. They must have come through.

She gave the giant Frosty a high-five as she walked back inside the barn to find Mom and Michelle. She spotted Michelle right off. She was offering cookies from a shiny silver platter to folks over near the gingerbread houses.

Folks cheered while playing carnival style games like the *Snowball Bash,* where players tried to hit milk bottles off bales of hay with foam snowballs. *Pin the Red Nose on the Reindeer* and a special ring toss over glittery miniature Christmas trees had the kids lined up ten deep for their chance to win a stuffed animal. The sputtering click clacking of the *Candy Cane Spinny Wheel* added a steady metronome to it all.

Adults and children alike shared in the joyous occasion, marveling at the huge Christmas tree, looking at the crafts tables of wreaths and stockings, and embracing the spirit of the holidays with hot chocolate and sugary treats.

Allie walked over to check out the gingerbread displays, one of her favorite parts. The huge gingerbread houses served as decoration in the booth where trays of home baked cookies were being passed around to everyone in attendance. Later, one of those gingerbread houses would receive the blue ribbon rosette and the honor of being the 48th Annual Evergreen Christmas Festival Gingerbread House. The winner's picture would be framed and hung next to the other forty-seven winners in Town Hall.

"They look delicious!" Michelle said as she took another tray to pass out. She turned to passersby to offer them a treat. "Take any one you want."

Hannah waved from near the spinning wheel. Allie waved back then caught Michelle by the elbow. "Congratulations, Michelle."

Her smile was ear to ear. "Thanks! I think we actually pulled it off...with a little help from a snow globe, of course." She set down the tray of cookies.

"Of course." Allie was so glad to see Michelle back to her old self.

"What about you, Hannah?" Michelle asked. "Any developments on the wish you made?"

Hannah blushed. "Shhh, no! Mine was just a silly wish anyway."

"Oh?" Allie nudged her, wanting to hear more.

"She's looking for someone who loves Christmas as much as she does," Michelle said.

"You deserve to find that," Allie said as they walked over to where Santa would be arriving soon.

But no sooner had the words come out of her mouth than a man about Hannah's age bumped into her, nearly knocking her off her feet.

"Oh!" Hannah squealed as he caught her by the arm, steadying her before she could fall.

And not only was he very handsome, but he was

wearing the very same royal blue Christmas sweater Hannah had on.

"Oh, sorry. I'm so sorry…" the man said.

Allie couldn't believe two people who didn't even know each other could possibly end up with a royal blue sweater with ho-ho-ho Santa in the middle surrounded by six appliqued snowflakes. If she hadn't just seen it with her own eyes, she'd never have believed it.

"Excuse me," Hannah said, but the man didn't move on. Instead he stood there seemingly entranced by Hannah.

"That's okay, it's…"

She glanced at his sweater, then tugged on her own, laughing when she realized they matched. "Hey?" She pointed to his, and he pointed to hers.

"I'm Hannah."

"Charlie."

Allie grabbed Michelle's arm. Was this what love at first sight looked like? Hannah must have truly wished for someone with all of her heart.

"Hi." Hannah's smile was contagious.

The man never took his eyes off of her, either. "Do you want to get some hot chocolate? Or apple cider?" Charlie pointed to the refreshments booth.

"Yeah," she said sweetly. "I'd love that." She flashed a hopeful grin toward Allie and Michelle as she followed him.

Michelle nudged Allie. That snow globe had come through again.

"Merry Christmas, everyone!" Carol held Joe's

hand, walking toward Michelle and Allie, with Henry and Ezra following along. "It's just magical!"

Michelle pulled her hands together like a prayer. "Henry, thank you for letting us do the festival here. You saved Christmas!"

"Ah, no…" Henry reveled in the idea of it all. "You think?"

Michelle nodded in appreciation.

"Michelle, everything looks amazing," Joe said.

"Thanks." She was enjoying all of the cheer around her.

"Isn't it amazing, Ezra?" Joe encouraged a response.

"Well, actually, there's…" Ezra wrinkled his forehead, almost grimacing, then busted out into a big smile. "Not a single thing I'd change."

"There you go," Allie said.

Maybe Michelle and Ezra would find a common ground after all. There was no doubt this year's festival was the best ever, and it wasn't the same old festival either. The new location and last-minute changes had worked out for the best, giving both Ezra and Michelle their way.

"And," Ezra said, spinning around and focusing on Allie, "I just heard the great news that Evergreen's veterinarian is staying put."

"Yes, she is." It was as if a million pounds had been lifted from her. Unpacking was going to be a welcome task.

"I just wish we could've convinced that doctor to stay," Ezra said.

That empty spot near her heart ached. "Yeah, me too." *If I'd been braver... If I'd said something to Ryan about what I was feeling... Could things have turned out differently?* "But he's probably in Florida by now." She gulped, an enormous sadness taking over her mood.

Mom clung to Dad's arm. Allie would be lucky to find a love like theirs someday.

"Ho, ho, ho." Nick, in full Santa gear, came into the barn chasing away her sorrow. He climbed to the stage in front of the huge holiday throne, carrying a big red bag piped in glittery gold. "Merry Christmas," he shouted with a wave of his arm.

Children and adults edged closer to the stage, cheering and shouting.

"Woo-hoo," Allie yelled.

"Santa has presents!" He sat in the huge wooden chair, with the rich red velvet upholstery and his initials in gold at the top. "Children first!" He opened the bag, and kids lined up on either side of him to get their surprises. The adults watched as Santa handed out presents, encouraging best behavior for another year.

Allie slipped outside for some air. The sky was clear, a million stars twinkling above giving the holiday decor inside the barn a run for best in show. She tugged her wool jacket tighter around her, finally feeling at home. Where she was supposed to be.

"Merry Christmas, Allie," Nick said.

She spun around. "Oh, Merry Christmas, Santa."

She must've been out here longer than she'd expected. "You were great in there. The kids love you."

His cheeks rose as he smiled, making his eyes seem to shimmer under his fluffy white eyebrows. "They are the true spirit of Christmas, but I have to ask you. Did your Christmas wish come true?"

"Oh? I think it did." She nodded, then shrugged. "Maybe not in the way that I hoped, but I think I learned something."

"And what's that, my dear?" The white fuzzy ball on the end of his red hat swung over his shoulder.

"Sometimes you end up exactly where you're supposed to be."

"I guess that's why it's called Christmas magic."

"Maybe," she said. "Can I offer you a ride into town?"

With a twinkle in his eye, he said, "No. I have my own transportation." He laughed, then jogged off as spry as a teenager.

"Allie!" The voice came from beyond the big trees near the main lane.

She spun toward it—and then realized her wishful thinking was playing tricks on her. Melancholy settled over her like a dark cloud, but then she caught movement in her peripheral and saw Zoe running toward her.

Allie hoped it wasn't her imagination. She blinked only once, then Zoe was flinging herself into Allie's arms. "You came back!" Overcome with emotion, she choked the words out.

"We missed you," Zoe said.

She leaned back and looked into the girl's eyes. "I missed you, too." Her heart pounded as if she'd just spent an hour on the ice rink.

Ryan walked up. His expression soft. Inviting. Without a word, he smiled.

Hannah called from the barn door. "Zoe? You're here. Do you want to be in the choir still? We go on in a couple of minutes."

"Can I, Dad?"

"Go have fun," Ryan said.

Hannah led Zoe inside, and Allie took three steps back.

She cocked her head. "What are you doing here?" She was getting a second chance.

"Heard you might be looking for a small town doctor."

Her hopes soared. "Oh, careful." She checked to see who was around. "Don't let Ezra hear you say that. He'll never let you leave." Or maybe she should run and grab Ezra right now!

He raised his shoulder in an easy laugh.

Why are they here? "Did your flight get canceled again?"

"Yes." He nodded, then shook his head. "But that's not why we came back."

"It's not?" *Please say you're staying.*

"No. This has been completely unexpected and amazing...." his words were filled with raw emotion, "...a magical Christmas for both Zoe and me." He stopped, swallowing hard. "Because of you."

Me too. She wanted to savor every word he was saying, but she also wanted him to know she felt the same way. Before he could say anything else, she blurted out, "I'm not moving to Washington, D.C."

"I know."

"How?"

"Because this is where you're supposed to be."

He was right. How did he figure out so quickly what she had had to work so hard to find out?

"Allie, I don't know if this is where I'm supposed to be or not, but I need to find out." He stepped toward her. "Because something keeps bringing me back here." He was close enough to kiss her.

Playfully she tipped her chin toward him, her pulse rushing so fast she'd give the little drummer boy a run for his money. "Is it a magical Christmas snow globe?"

"Maybe."

Snow fell, and he pulled her close, pressing his lips to hers. She rose up on her toes, kissing him back.

As they took a breath, smiling into each other's eyes, the sound of jingling sleigh bells filled the night, followed by Santa exclaiming, "Ho, ho, ho. Merry Christmas."

It had almost sounded like Santa had flown across the sky above them. That was better than fireworks!

She laid the palm of her hand on Ryan's chest as he held her. Her heart completely filled with joy.

"Dashing through the snow..." rose from inside the barn.

"Let's go listen." Allie tugged him toward the joyous sound. "Come on."

They stepped inside, arm in arm.

Zoe waved from the middle of the small group of carolers.

Allie and Ryan both waved back.

Michelle, Barbara, and Ezra stood off to the side. Allie flashed them a smile of excitement, then overheard Michelle say to Ezra, "Looks like you got your doctor," as she lifted a big snowflake-shaped cookie to her lips.

Allie squeezed Ryan's arm. Yes. Dr. B would be the perfect addition to Evergreen. She looked up into his kind face. The perfect addition to her life.

The carolers finished with a resounding, "—one-horse open sleigh."

Applause filled the barn, echoing from the metal building like thunder.

"Oh my gosh," Ryan said, clapping with all the joy of a proud father.

Zoe beamed with pride on stage.

Allie had tears blurring her vision as the kids sang another song.

It couldn't be a more perfect Christmas Eve.

Chapter Twenty-Six

On Christmas day, Joe and Carol Shaw hosted a special holiday dinner at the Chris Kringle Kitchen for their closest friends and loved ones.

The stuffed turkey was baked to perfection and garnished with fresh seasonal fruits. Homemade gravy and cranberry sauce, potatoes both white and sweet, and everyone's favorite veggies and casseroles filled the long table.

Joe sat at the head of the table with Carol to his left and Barbara across from her. Hannah and her new beau Charlie sat across from each other in matching red holiday sweaters. Michelle and Ezra were still bickering, but mostly poking fun with each other now that the festival was behind them and it had been an amazing success.

Zoe, Ryan, and Allie all sat together at the end of the table, thankful for the wonderful blessings the holiday had brought. Ryan leaned over and kissed Allie, with the magical snow globe just behind them on the place of honor next to the register.

Joe raised his punch cup in the air. "A toast!"

They all followed suit.

"To family. To friends. To Evergreen," Joe said. A melodic wave of Merry Christmas wishes flowed across the table as their glasses met and rang.

Everyone agreed that the Christmas feast that year was truly special.

Surrounded by family and friends old and new, the spirit of the holidays was all around them. Ryan rose from the table and picked up the snow globe. He knew exactly what he'd be wishing for this year.

Epilogue

The banner for the 49th Annual Evergreen Christmas Festival hung high above the entrance of the barn at Henry Holloway's farm. Not the new barn like last year, but the *old* one. Henry's son and daughter-in-law had helped Henry move his operation into the new barn at the beginning of the year, and they'd taken over the old barn. They'd repurposed it into a wonderful rustic hall, The Barn at H2 Farms, for hosting parties, events, and weddings. It hadn't taken but two events for word to spread like wildfire about the great setting, and since they used all local vendors, the pricing was competitive, too. Already there were weddings and parties booked two and three years out. Plus, the town of Evergreen had signed a contract to have the Christmas Festival there for the next four years.

With more space at the new location, Ezra got his wish to add several new features for a *not-your-parents'-festival,* and Allie and Michelle agreed to co-chair the event.

Allie marked off two more tasks from the project plan. "Michelle, did you hear back from the guy with the camel? He was supposed to be here two hours ago."

"Yes. He called an hour ago," Michelle said. "He got slowed down in traffic and had to take a detour that took him out of cell phone range. He'll be here any minute."

"Thank goodness. People are so excited to see that camel." Allie had known a real-life camel would be a draw, but the interest had been crazy. People had been talking about it since the first day they'd advertised it. The camel was part of the live Nativity that would start at five o'clock, but parents were already asking to see it three hours early.

"I know." Michelle cocked her head. "But I'm going to tell you right now, I'm keeping my distance from that giant thing. You couldn't cast me in that live Nativity scene with live animals for all the cookies in Connecticut."

"Oh, come on. They're all pets. You'd be fine."

"*You'd* be fine," Michelle said. "I'd be terrified."

"Well, no worries, because you don't have to be near any of the livestock. That's my area."

"Good."

"I think we've got everything ready, then." Allie double-checked her project plan again. "I need to run on over to the petting zoo and check in on Zoe. She's with Snowflake over there."

"Sure thing. I'll hold down things in here."

"Hey, you two," Ezra said as he walked into their temporary office in the barn. "How's everything?"

"Right on schedule, Ezra," Michelle said.

"Excellent. I'm going to do a live Internet broadcast for the app." He ran his fingers through his hair.

Michelle laughed, and Allie knew what was going through her best friend's mind. They'd finally had to compromise and let Ezra run with his big mobile app idea. Allie had to admit that the app had turned out to be helpful. They'd even sold tickets through it this year. Plus, the project had kept Ezra out of their hair for the most part, since he was managing the app for the town until they could one day afford to compensate someone to do it.

"Come on. You two get in here. I want you to be in the feed." Without giving them a moment to protest, he held up his phone in selfie mode, standing right in front of them with his arm extended. The flash came on, and he started talking.

"Mayor Ezra Green here on sight at The Barn at H2 Farms for the 49th Evergreen Christmas Festival which kicked off just a couple of hours ago with games and a petting zoo for the kids. The live Nativity scene will be in place at five o'clock, and the festival will be in full swing by six. Get your family and friends together, and come on out and enjoy the fun before Santa comes tonight." He turned the camera angle toward Allie and Michelle. "And be sure to thank these two lovely ladies, Dr. Allie Shaw and Michelle Lansing, when you see them. This festival would not be the success it is without these two working tirelessly for the people of Evergreen and our neighboring communities. This is Mayor Ezra Green saying Merry Christmas. See you soon!"

Allie had to give it to Ezra. He'd brought a new energy to this town, and he was turning out to be a good mayor.

"Thanks!" Ezra put his phone in his pocket. "I'm going to get this up on the Internet. You two were great."

"That man has more energy…" Michelle said.

"Yeah, yeah. But at least that app has kept him pretty much out of our way. For that, I'm forever grateful."

"You've got a point." Michelle drew a cross in the air. "I take it back."

"I'm out of here." Allie walked out to the far end of the barn where the panels had been set up for the petting zoo. Old gumball machines were filled with animal food for the kids to feed the animals. 4H and FFA students were on hand to help out, answer questions and ensure a safe environment for the animals and the visitors.

Allie passed a pen of goats, one with chickens, one with a couple of Henry's draft horses, and one with sheep. Buttercup had her own stall, too.

In the next stall, Zoe stood next to Snowflake.

She'd put a bright red ribbon around the calf's neck, and she wore a matching one in her hair.

She watched as Zoe talked to a group of children about Snowflake. About being here the day Snowflake was born and all the things she'd been working with Snowflake on over the year. She talked about how much weight Snowflake had gained and shared general bovine facts, too.

Allie was so proud of her. They'd signed her up for 4H this year and she'd shown Snowflake at the county fair, taking first place in the novice showmanship class.

Today, Zoe displayed confidence about the information she was sharing.

Zoe noticed her standing behind the other parents and paused to give Allie an animated wave.

Allie blew her a kiss followed by a thumb's up.

A woman standing nearby nudged Allie's arm. "That's my little boy right there. We're from Montpelier. He's never been this close to a real cow before. Your daughter is amazing. So intelligent, and kind. You must be so proud."

She started to correct her about her relationship with Zoe, but then didn't. "Thank you. We're very proud of her." She couldn't be prouder if she was her own daughter.

A warm hand slipped under Allie's arm and around her waist from behind. "Hello, Dr. Shaw," Ryan whispered into her ear.

She turned into his arms. "Hello, Dr. B."

"How's it going?"

"Fabulous."

He dropped a kiss on her nose.

"Zoe is doing great," she said.

"You've taught her a lot about animals this year," he said. "She's a natural."

"She is."

Zoe led the children out of the petting area and locked the stall behind her. "Hey, Dad!"

"Hey, kiddo. I hear you did a great job. I'm sorry I missed it."

"That's okay," Zoe said.

The same woman who'd spoken to Allie earlier came over. "Young lady, I want to tell you that you were very informative. I was just telling your mother how impressed I was. Thank you for making today extra special for us."

"You're welcome," Zoe said politely.

The woman walked away, and Allie felt her skin flush. "I'm sorry. I should've corrected her when she said something to me. That I'm not her mom. I—"

"That's okay." Zoe took Allie's hand. "You're like a mom to me."

Allie pulled her hand to her heart.

"Zoe and I have talked about that." He looked lovingly in Allie's direction.

Her eyes teared up. "Thank you. That's so sweet to say. Such a wonderful compliment." Her phone pinged. The text was to let her know the camel had arrived. "I have to go check the camel in. What time are we going home to decorate the tree?"

"Seven o'clock," Zoe said. "Right after Santa leaves."

"Perfect." Allie waved, leaving Zoe and Ryan behind.

The live Nativity began right on time. Music played as the actors and animals took their positions. People were already snapping pictures and talking about how wonderful it was. A bright star hung high in the sky above the manger. It was truly magical.

The announcement came over the loud speaker that Santa had been sighted, and shortly thereafter the sound of sleigh bells filled the hall. Then Nick, dressed as Santa, stepped out onto the stage.

At seven o'clock sharp, Allie, Ryan and Zoe met at the *Snowball Bash* station.

"Everyone ready to go?" Ryan asked.

"We are," Allie said, holding tight to Zoe's hand. "My parents just said they're going to come over and help. You don't mind, do you?"

"Mind?" Ryan asked. "Of course not. The more, the merrier."

"Great. Thanks. This is the best Christmas ever."

Ryan wrapped his arms around Allie and Zoe. "I couldn't agree more."

When they got to her house, they turned on the Christmas music and started trimming the tree. They'd already decorated a tree at Ryan's and in both the veterinarian clinic and Ryan's office weeks ago, but they'd saved this one as a Christmas Eve tradition. Where it had all begun.

Allie's parents came in the door. "Hey, honey. We brought dessert."

"Of course you did," she teased. Mom was always bringing food over.

Zoe ran over to them and gave them a hug.

The five of them gathered in the living room, each taking a turn placing an ornament on the tree. One at a time, the tree began to transform.

Carol pulled Allie aside. "Allie, you know my wish on the snow globe took a while, but it's come true."

"You mean the one about you wanting a baby girl and getting me?" She'd heard that story a million times.

"No. A new wish. That you'd find the right man and have a daughter of your own. Just like you. You have Ryan now, and Zoe is just like you were at that age." Carol hugged Allie's arm. "I'm so happy for you, dear. I knew that snow globe would come through." She nudged Allie's arm. "Maybe I should wish for a son someday too."

"Don't rush things, Mom." But Allie would be lying if she didn't admit that she'd allowed herself to dream about that, too. "But thank you for wishing on the snow globe." She looked over at Ryan helping Zoe place an ornament high on the tree. Allie had never imagined this kind of happiness. "I love them so much."

Carol's eyes teared up. "Chopping onions," she pleaded.

"Right, Mom."

Ryan turned down the music. "This is a perfect night. I'm so glad we're all here together to decorate the tree, and to celebrate Christmas together. I bought something new for the tree." He pulled a big, glossy white box from behind the chair.

"How did you sneak that in?" Allie asked.

"My secret," Ryan said, sending Zoe into giggles. He opened the box and lifted a beautiful white angel tree topper from inside.

Allie and Carol exclaimed in harmony, "She's beautiful."

"I was hoping you'd like her," Ryan said.

Zoe grinned. "I helped pick her out."

"I love it. I do. She's perfect." Allie's heart overflowed with love tonight.

"Come on, Zoe. Let's get you up here to do the honors. Allie, you spot her. She's grown a lot since last year." Ryan lifted Zoe to his shoulders.

Allie walked over and placed a hand on Zoe's knee to spot her.

Zoe held the angel and leaned toward the tree, then the angel went toppling right into Allie's hands.

"Oops," Zoe said.

Ryan stooped to the floor so Zoe could get down.

"It's okay. I've got her." Allie handed the angel back to Zoe.

"Wait." Zoe's face showed confusion. "Something's wrong with her."

"Did she break?" Allie rushed in to check. When she did, she realized that wired to the perfect halo on the angel's head was a diamond eternity ring.

Allie looked at Ryan, who was smiling, then to her mother, who had tears streaming down her cheeks and was clapping her hands together. "Is this...?" She couldn't believe her eyes.

Ryan stepped over and took her hands into his. "Zoe and I have something to ask you, Allie."

"We're already a family," Zoe said. "We love being here in Evergreen with you. And Dad's back with his patients and spending more time with me. I feel like the luckiest girl in the world. I don't ever want this to change."

"I—" Allie put her hand to her heart, which felt like it was going to beat right out of her chest. She sucked in a breath.

"Allie, I know this is soon," Ryan said. "But if there's one thing I've learned, it's that sometimes you can't plan for things too far out. There's an expiration date on everything, even life. We just don't know what it is." His face was serious, but his eyes were filled with love. "I want to spend the rest of my life making every single day the very best one possible for you and for Zoe."

Zoe had taken the ring off of the halo. She handed it to her dad.

"I hope this isn't too soon for you. If it is, I understand." He glanced over at Zoe. "We understand.

But I'd love to make this official. I'd love nothing more than for you to be Mrs. B…"

"And stepmom to me." Zoe clasped her hands together. "Please say yes, Allie."

Allie brought both hands to her face, tears of joy springing to her cheeks. "You knew," she said to her mom and dad.

"We did." They were both smiling and were teared up, too.

"Yes." She turned to Ryan, and looked into Zoe's sweet face. "Yes. I want to be your wife. Zoe's stepmother. Live each day to the fullest with both of you for the rest of our lives."

Ryan pulled her into his arms and kissed her, then slipped the ring on her finger.

"Come on, kiddo." He lifted Zoe, and she placed the angel on top of the tree. He put her down next to him.

"I love you both," Allie said.

"You. This. Our love." Ryan said to her. "Us being together as a family here in Evergreen. This was my wish on the snow globe last year. My heart truly wanted it."

"Mine does, too." Allie rose to her toes and kissed him, so thankful for snow globe wishes being granted.

And it lived on, for many yuletide seasons to come—but perhaps those are stories for another time. Until then, hold tight to the magic of Christmas…you never know when the next wish might come true.

Vermont Christmas Card Cookies
A Hallmark Original Recipe

In *Christmas in Evergreen*, snowy weather—and wishes on a magic snow globe—lead Ryan and Zoe to an idyllic small town in Vermont. As they help Allie make her favorite frosted sugar cookies for the town festival, they get caught up in the joy of the season. Whether you make our Vermont Christmas Tree Cookies with friends or family, or you share them with the people you love, they'll give you that warm, Christmas-y feeling, too.

Yield: 3 dozen cookies
Prep Time: 75 minutes
Cook Time: 45 minutes
Total Time: 2 hours

INGREDIENTS

Soft Sugar Cookies:
- 2 cups (4 sticks) unsalted butter, room temperature
- 2 cups granulated sugar
- 2 large eggs, room temperature
- 1 ½ tablespoons vanilla extract
- 1 teaspoon orange extract
- 6 cups flour
- 1 tablespoon baking powder
- 1 teaspoon kosher salt

Vanilla Buttercream Frosting:
- 1 cup (2 sticks) unsalted butter, room temperature
- 4 cups confectioner's sugar, sifted
- ¼ cup heavy whipping cream
- 1 tablespoon vanilla extract
- Assorted food coloring (various shades of green)
- 4 piping bags fitted with an assortment of tips
- Assorted sizes white pearl nonpareils
- White sparkling sugar

DIRECTIONS

1. Preheat oven to 350 degrees F.

2. To prepare sugar cookies: cream butter and sugar in the bowl of a stand mixer with paddle attachment on medium speed until fluffy. Add eggs one at a time and mix until completely incorporated. Scrape down sides of bowl; add vanilla and orange extracts and mix until blended.

3. Sift flour, baking powder and salt into a separate bowl; slowly add to mixing bowl on low speed until fully blended and dough pulls away from sides of bowl. Divide dough into 2 pieces.

4. On a 12-inch x 16½-inch non-stick silicone baking mat or parchment paper, roll out half of dough to ¼-inch thickness. Place baking mat or parchment on a cookie sheet and chill dough in freezer for 5 minutes. (Freezing dough slightly makes it easier to cut out shapes and transfer to cookie sheets.)

5. Remove dough from freezer. Cut out shapes with a variety of Christmas tree-shaped cookie cutters. Arrange on a cookie sheet and bake for 15 minutes. Remove from oven and cool. Repeat with remaining dough.

6. To prepare buttercream frosting: cream butter in the bowl of a stand mixer with paddle

attachment on medium speed until fluffy. Slowly add confectioner's sugar and beat on low speed until smooth, scraping down sides of bowl after partially blended. Add cream and vanilla extract and beat until smooth.

7. Divide buttercream frosting into 4 portions. Tint each portion to desired shade with food coloring and transfer to a pastry bag.

8. Using a variety of tips, pipe buttercream frosting on cooled sugar cookies to resemble tree branches. Decorate frosted cookies with sparkling sugar and pearls. If making ahead, refrigerate cookies to hold.

Thanks so much for reading *Christmas in Evergreen*. We hope you enjoyed it!

You might like these other books from Hallmark Publishing:

Journey Back to Christmas
Christmas in Homestead
Love You Like Christmas
A Heavenly Christmas
A Dash of Love
Love Locks
The Perfect Catch
Like Cats and Dogs
Dater's Handbook

For information about our new releases and exclusive offers, sign up for our free newsletter at hallmarkchannel.com/hallmark-publishing-newsletter

You can also connect with us here:

Facebook.com/HallmarkPublishing

Twitter.com/HallmarkPublish

About The Author

USA Today bestselling author Nancy Naigle whips up small-town love stories with a whole lot of heart. She began her popular contemporary romance series Adams Grove while juggling a successful career in finance and life on a seventy-six-acre goat farm. Along with the Adams Grove series, she is also the author of the Boot Creek Novels, G Team Mysteries, and several standalone novels, including *Christmas Joy*, a heartwarming holiday story coming to the Hallmark Channel as part of their holiday programming. Now happily retired from a career in the financial industry, she devotes her time to writing, horseback riding, and enjoying the occasional spa day. A Virginia girl at heart, Nancy now calls North Carolina home.